D1601694

MURDEROUS
BETRAYAL

MURDEROUS
BETRAYAL

M A COMLEY

2018

New York Times and USA Today bestselling author M A Comley
Published by Jeamel Publishing limited
Copyright © 2018 M A Comley
Digital Edition, License Notes

ISBN-13: 978-1719557276

ISBN-10: 1719557276

OTHER BOOKS BY M A COMLEY

KEEP IN TOUCH WITH THE AUTHOR

Twitter
https://twitter.com/Melcom1

Blog
http://melcomley.blogspot.com

Facebook
http://smarturl.it/sps7jh

Newsletter
http://smarturl.it/8jtcvv

BookBub
www.bookbub.com/authors/m-a-comley

ACKNOWLEDGMENTS

Thank you as always to my rock, Jean, who keeps me supplied with endless cups of coffee while I punish my keyboard. I'd be lost without you in my life.

Special thanks as always go to my talented editor, Stefanie Spangler Buswell and to Karri Klawiter for her superb cover design expertise.

My heartfelt thanks go to my wonderful proofreader Joseph for spotting all the lingering nits.

And finally, to all the wonderful Bloggers and Facebook groups for their never-ending support of my work.

You're always in my thoughts Mary.

PROLOGUE

"I'm just going in now. I'll see you at the pub later, buy you a beer to help celebrate your good news. A grandfather again—you'll have quite a tribe to babysit for soon, old man."

"Funny. I bloody well hope not. Six grandkids are more than enough for a man of my age to keep up with. I just wish I was ten years younger."

"Gotta fly. It's raining, and I'm getting wet. See you soon." Paul Potts ended the call to his brother and entered the communal area of the flats he owned in a district of Bristol. He inhaled a large breath. He was there to collect a couple of rents that were overdue. He'd given the three tenants enough time to get the funds together, and he was about to get tough. He hated being crappy with his tenants, but he was running a business, not a charity. He had his own bills to pay, just like everyone else.

Unfortunately, some of his tenants had recently lost their jobs and hadn't received their payments from the Social yet. He knew that took a few weeks to sort out, so he'd given them three weeks' grace already. Now he wanted his money. With his heart pounding, he approached the first door and knocked on it three times.

"Yeah, who is it?" a stern voice asked from behind the closed door.

"Mr. Hawkins, it's Paul Potts. I've come to collect the rent you owe me."

"Hey, man. When the Social pay me, then I'll pay you. You have my assurance about that."

"Open the door, Mr. Hawkins."

He heard the chain being removed, and the door eased open. "What more can I say? You'll get your money as soon as I can physically put it in your hand."

"Have you been down the Social to chase them?"

"Yeah, man, like every bloody day. You know what a bunch of tossers they are. Jesus, what more can I do? If I was a lass, I could go out there and spread my legs for a few quid, but I'm not."

"There's no need for you to speak to me like that. I'll give you until the end of the week."

Hawkins glared at him through narrowed eyes. "Threats ain't going to help the situation, either. I'm doing my best. You've just got to be more patient."

"For your information, I'm a very patient man, but you've got to get off your arse and get down there. Make a nuisance of yourself. I have a list of people needing a room. It's not fair to keep them on the waiting list."

"Yeah, well, I don't think it would be very fair of you to kick me out, either. The fault lies with the Soc, not me. Give me a break, man."

"I am. You've got until the end of the week."

Hawkins's lip turned up at the side, and he slammed the door in Paul's face.

Crap! One down, only two more to go! I hate this side of things. The money just ain't worth the bloody hassle.

He trudged up the stairs to the next floor and knocked on the second door in the tiny dark hallway. He looked up at the light overhead and made a mental note to replace the bulb from the box he carried in his car before he left for the evening. The door remained unanswered, so he thumped his fist on it again.

After a few seconds, the door opened. Stuart Rawlinson had obviously just woken up. His ginger hair was a mess, and his eyes seemed to be unfocused as he struggled to see who was standing before him. Paul recognised the strange smell coming from inside the flat as cannabis.

"Hey, how's it diddling, Paul?"

"Not so good, Stuart. You're gonna hate me, but I've come for the rent you owe me."

Rawlinson held his arms out to the side and shrugged. "The truth is, I ain't got two ha'pennies to rub together."

Paul sighed. That was clearly a lie as the man had recently taken drugs. The evidence was clear. "That's a shame, Stuart. Then I'm going to have to ask you to vacate the flat immediately."

14

Rawlinson shook his head and stuck it forward as if to focus more on Paul. "What? You can't do that."

"I'm afraid I can. It's in your rental agreement, the one you signed the day you moved in. Look, as much as I like to help you guys out, I'm not running a damn charity here. Three of you owe me rent this month. This can't go on. If you've got money for drugs, then you've damn well got enough to pay the rent."

"The drugs were a gift from a mate, man. I swear they were. I'll get you your money by the end of the week. I promise."

"You better, or you'll be on the streets. That's *my* promise to you." Paul turned away before Stuart could say another word. He flinched when the door slammed shut behind him. He carried on up the next flight of stairs to the top floor of the house and banged on the final door.

Bob Nuttall opened it instantly. "Hi, Paul. Before you start, I should have your money in a few days. You know how it is. I've got a cash-flow problem, mate."

Paul shook his head. His blood was boiling as the anger flooded through him. "Yeah, haven't we all? Look, you're the third one in this block to let me down. That in itself gives me a cash-flow problem. I'll tell you what I've just told the bloody others. I'm not running a damn charity here. Either you pay up, or you ship out. I've got a long waiting list of people who want to pay for these flats. Get your bloody act together and get the money to me within the next few days, or you'll be out on the street. Is that clear enough for you, *mate*?"

"Yep, loud and clear. I'm gonna bust a gut to get your money to you within a few days. Thanks for being so understanding."

Paul snorted. "Understanding? Seriously, you guys are going to cause me to have a heart attack, the amount of stress you put me under. You do realise that next month's rent will be due in a few weeks, right? How the hell are you going to pay that on time?"

"I will. I promise you, I will."

"You better. I'm not going to have this every damn month. Bloody hell, I took you guys in when other landlords refused to open their doors to you—big mistake on my part. Lesson learnt. I won't put myself in this situation again. I can assure you. I'll open my doors to female tenants next time. You men just aren't worth trying to help because you insist on taking the piss."

Bob shrugged. "What do you expect me to say to that? You'll have your money in a few days as promised." He slammed the door in Paul's face.

Paul retraced his steps down the two flights of stairs and pulled up the collar on his jacket before he stepped out the front door. His car was about fifty feet up the road. Before braving the weather, he paused and waited to see if the rain eased a little. When it didn't look like it had intention of relenting, he hunkered down into his collar and ran towards the car. No sooner had he left the steps to the building than something heavy struck his neck. He instantly lost his balance and tumbled to the ground. Another blow to his head knocked him out.

~ ~ ~

When Paul woke up, he didn't have a clue where he was or how long he'd been unconscious. He tried to sit up in the darkness and banged his head. He was in a confined space, and there was the smell of petrol close by. His head was woozy, making it difficult for him to think straight. He was moving. He felt a little motion sickness... or was that because of the bang he'd received to his head? It was a few minutes before his situation became clearer. He felt around himself and found a tow rope and a petrol canister. He was sure he was in the boot of a car—his own car.

What the hell is going on? He was unsure whether to bang on the boot or not, afraid that might anger the person who had intentionally knocked him out and abducted him. *Damn, what am I supposed to do now?*

The car's speed increased. *Does that mean we're on an open road? A motorway, perhaps?* He tried to think if he had anything useful around him that he could use to try to jemmy the boot open, but nothing came to mind. All he could do was lie there and wait for the car to stop. Still, he wasn't sure how he would proceed even when that happened. *Who would do this to me? Why would they do this to me?*

Time marched on until the car's speed finally decreased. He banged his head on the boot as the terrain became bumpy. *What the fuck? What the hell is going on?*

The car stopped. He heard a door open and slam shut and braced himself to meet his abductor. Then he thought he heard another car arrive and a second door bang. *Are there two of them?* He wasn't sure as his head was still too muzzy.

Still no one came to see how he was. Suddenly, the car began to move. He heard laughter in the distance. The ground was bumpier than before, and his head continuously hit the sides and the top of the boot. *Jesus, what the hell is happening?* He was disorientated, and the only thing he was certain of was that the car had changed angles as if it were going downhill. The speed increased. With nothing to steady him, the force of the car's momentum turned him around until he was wedged up against the back seats. He tried to push at them, but they refused to budge. As the car's speed appeared to double, he quickly realised that he was plunging to his death.

"Please… please help me! I don't want to die like this. Help me!"

A large thud ended his cries for help. He slipped into unconsciousness as water flooded into the boot of the car.

CHAPTER ONE

Kayli woke up and stretched out a hand. Panic gripped her when she found the other side of the bed was empty. She sat upright and pulled the quilt up to her chin as she ran through the events of the previous night. She let out a relieved sigh when thoughts of her and Mark making love filled her mind. Hearing a noise from downstairs, she realised he was in the kitchen, hopefully throwing some breakfast together.

For a moment, Kayli thought she'd woken up in a parallel universe where Mark was missing again. She never ever wanted to be in that situation again. She'd very nearly lost the man she loved once, and she wasn't about to let it happen a second time.

Mark entered the room. His handsome features stretched into the warmest of smiles. "Good morning, precious. How are you on this bright, crisp November morning?"

"Wow, this is a surprise. Breakfast in bed. What have I done to deserve this?"

He placed the tray next to her on the bed and leaned in for a lingering kiss. "I thought I'd make the effort, what with this being your first day back at work."

"You're a treasure. Wish I didn't have to go back. Having you to myself for the last week has been wonderful, just what the doctor ordered, eh?"

Mark looked down at the pink slashes on his torso. The wounds inflicted by the Taliban were healing fast, thankfully. "I'll be okay. The scars will always be a reminder of how much you love me."

She kissed him again. "You bet. I hope they begin to fade soon, though." Kayli looked down at the feast he'd prepared. "Yum, a full English. I never knew you had it in you to create such a delight."

His eyebrows wiggled. "There's a lot about me you don't know, darling."

"Hmm… I look forward to you revealing what that means over the coming years. What's on your agenda today?"

"Your dad has summoned me to the house this morning. Should I go in a suit?"

She chuckled. "Don't be silly. Just go in your jeans, as usual." She placed a forkful of toast and beans into her mouth.

"I have an inkling you know what this meeting is about. Do I have to tickle you to get the information out of you?"

"Oh heck, I promised I wouldn't spoil the surprise. I think he has a few job interviews lined up for you."

"That's excellent news. I really didn't relish going back out to Afghanistan to fulfil my contract with the security firm."

"Or spend your time down at the jobcentre, either, I should imagine."

"That too. Eat up. Otherwise, you're going to be late on your first day back."

Kayli ate her breakfast in record time then shot out of bed and into the bathroom. She emerged ten minutes later with mixed emotions. On the one hand, she felt invigorated, and on the other, she was nervous about what her father had lined up for Mark. She hoped it wasn't something as dangerous as his last role.

"I need to fly now. Don't want to be late. Will you ring me later, let me know how you got on with Dad?"

Mark approached her, wrapped his arms around her and kissed the top of her head. "Of course. Hope work goes well for you today. What do you want for dinner?"

"You don't have to do that. We'll get a takeaway tonight for a treat."

"Indian or Chinese?"

She chuckled. "We'll decide later. Not sure I can make that decision on a full stomach."

"Fair point. Have a good day."

Kayli left the house in good spirits and drove to the police station with an upbeat CD playing in the car to match her mood. She arrived just as her partner, DS Dave Chaplin, was struggling to get out of his vehicle. "Need a hand, partner?"

"Sorry, I didn't see you there. I'm good, thanks. Another week, and I should be free of this damn cast."

Kayli looked down at his stiff leg and the crutches holding him upright. "That soon? Hey, I think you've coped really well. Did you miss me?"

"Not really. The question is, did you miss us?"

Kayli shook her head and tutted. "Hardly, Dave. I was on honeymoon. I have to admit this place never entered my mind while I was—"

He raised a hand to stop her. "Umm… no offence, boss, but stop right there. I don't need to hear all the gruesome details."

"Plonker. Come on, I'll race you up the stairs."

He shook his head. "You're such a scream at times. You missed your vocation. You should have been on the stage with that sparkling wit… not."

She rushed ahead of him to open the door to the entrance then left him navigating the stairs to the first floor while she ran ahead to buy the coffees. DC Donna Travis and DC Graeme Chance were both already sitting at their desks when she pushed open the door to the incident room. "Morning, Donna and Graeme. Eager beavers this morning, aren't we?"

"We thought we'd catch up on the paperwork from the last case we solved, boss, before another one lands on our desks," Donna said.

"Very wise. What was the case?" she asked, slotting a coin in the vending machine.

"Nothing major. Well, it was to the victim, of course. A GBH charge—a man was set upon by a group of thugs outside a nightclub late at night."

"I take it you managed to track down the culprits?"

"Yes, Graeme worked his magic on the nightclub's CCTV footage. Some of us recognised a few of the gang members, and the arrests soon followed. One of our easier cases to solve, shall we say. How's married life treating you?"

"No complaints from me so far, Donna. Thanks for asking." Kayli inserted another coin in the machine just as a breathless Dave hobbled through the door.

"Damn stairs get steeper every day," he complained, collapsing into his chair.

"Maybe you're just not as fit as you used to be, mate." Kayli winked at him and placed a coffee on his desk.

He waved his crutch at her and dropped it to the floor. "I'd like to see how you'd cope with having to deal with these guys for six weeks."

Kayli bit down on her tongue. "Okay, I'll give you that one." She turned to walk into her office. "I'll be tackling the dross on my desk if anyone needs me."

She opened her office door, stuck her head into the room and almost backed out again when she saw not one, but two mountains of paperwork awaiting her. "Oh bugger! Is it worth taking a week off if this is what I have to contend with when I get back?"

"To be fair, boss, that's three weeks' worth of paperwork, not just one," Donna said from behind her.

"You're right, of course. Damn, by the looks of things, I'm going to be here until midnight every day."

"Want me to give you a hand after I've completed the paperwork on the other case?"

"Might be a good idea. Thanks for the offer, Donna. I'll sort it into stacks first, categorising it into urgent and non-urgent piles."

"Call me when you need a hand," Donna said before she left the office again.

Kayli didn't get very far before the phone on her desk rang. "DI Bright. Can I help?"

"Morning, ma'am. It's Ray."

Kayli frowned. "What is it, Ray?"

He lowered his voice and explained, "Umm... sorry to trouble you, ma'am, but I've got a distant friend of mine down here, and I wondered if you could help him."

"Regarding what, Ray? A crime?"

He inhaled a large breath. "You know I wouldn't normally involve you if I didn't think it was important. My friend's brother went missing a few days ago."

"Sorry about that, Ray, but we have a missing persons department whose team is better equipped than I am to deal with such matters."

"I appreciate that, ma'am. It's just that it's out of character for his brother not to be in contact with Samuel. To me, I'm getting the impression that something far more sinister has occurred, although I wouldn't dare say that to him. You know how it goes when something doesn't sit right with you. This is one of those times."

"All right, you win. Do you want to put your friend in an interview room and I'll come down in a minute or two?"

"Thank you, ma'am. I'll do that."

Kayli ended the call and left her desk. She entered the incident room and walked towards Donna's desk. "Grab your notebook and come with me, Donna."

Dave cocked his head and looked puzzled. "Is something wrong?"

"I need to interview someone before I can determine that, partner. You stay here. I'll take Donna with me rather than see you struggle down the stairs and back up again so soon."

"Thanks for thinking of me." Dave grinned.

Kayli and Donna trotted down the stairs to Ray's desk. "What room, Ray?"

"Room One, ma'am. Thanks for this. He's a little distraught, which is unlike him."

"No problem. Let's see what he has to say. Have you given him a drink?"

"Yes, ma'am."

"Good." Kayli turned and walked down the narrow corridor to the room at the end, with Donna close behind her. She opened the door to find a grey-haired gentleman sitting at the desk, his head bowed, clutching his hands together in front of him. "Mr. Potts, I'm DI Kayli Bright, and this is DC Donna Travis. She'll be taking notes throughout this interview if that's all right with you."

He rose from his chair and stood until Kayli and Donna were seated opposite him. "Of course. Thank you for seeing me at such short notice. I didn't know who else to turn to. My wife suggested contacting Ray. He's an old mate of mine. That's why I'm here, really."

"We'll do our very best to assist you, sir. Why don't you start from the beginning? When was the last time you either saw your brother or heard from him?"

"Two days ago. We had made arrangements to go to the pub together, except he didn't show up."

Kayli checked to make sure Donna was taking notes. "I take it that's unusual?"

"Yes. I spoke to him around six thirty that evening, and he told me he would be at the pub later. When he didn't show up, I presumed he'd changed his mind and gone home."

"I take it you didn't ring him to find out?"

"No. To be honest, a couple of my mates and I got involved in a game of bridge, and before we knew it, it was eleven thirty, and the landlord was kicking us out. I thought it was too late to ring him when I got home, but I tried first thing the next morning. Both his house phone and his mobile remained unanswered. It's so unlike him."

"I see. When you last spoke to him, can you tell me where he was?"

Samuel nodded. "Oh yes. He was at the flats he owns, collecting back rent from the tenants."

"Can you give us that address?"

"Lexington Road, number twelve."

Kayli scratched her head as she thought. "Is that in the Clifton area?"

"That's right. It's a bit of a dive, but the council are about to start renovating some of the houses down there, so that should help the property prices rise in the area. Sorry, I sound like a bloody estate agent. What I'm trying to say is that's why Paul took a gamble on the property. The trouble is that the only tenants he could attract were ones sitting on the dole. I warned him not to go ahead with purchasing the property, but once my brother gets a notion in his head, it's a devil of a job trying to dissuade him."

"How long has your brother owned the property?"

"About a year. Sadly, his wife died of lung cancer. He used her insurance policy money to buy the property in the hope that the income would subsidise him in the future. Let's face it—the state pension isn't up to much nowadays, is it?"

23

"That's true. Has your brother had any problems with the tenants at the property?"

His mouth turned down at the sides, and he shook his head. "Not really, not apart from them falling behind on the rent, that is. I told him he should have employed an agency to deal with that side of things, but the silly bugger was too tight to hand over the ten per cent fee these guys demand."

"I can understand that. How has your brother been since he lost his wife?"

"He's been all right lately. After she died, he found it a struggle to get through his days, but the kids did their best to help him handle his grief."

"Kids? How many?"

"Three in total. One of his own and two stepchildren. Maureen was married before, and she brought Sharon and Dylan into the marriage. Can I put it that way? It sounds funny. Anyway, not long after they got married, Anita was born."

"Was Maureen pregnant before they married?"

"Sorry, no. What I meant to say was Anita came along nine months or so after they tied the knot. They had a whirlwind romance, met and married within a month. They truly loved the bones of each other. Never seen two people more in love, if you must know. Which is why he struggled after Maureen died. I'm not saying he would have done anything daft like suicide. He loved Anita too much to put her through that. If she hadn't been around, though, I think he might have contemplated it."

"Does Anita live at home still?"

"Yes, she's still there. She looks after him, or I should say they look after each other. Anita took on all the domestic chores like cooking and cleaning while Paul sees to the garden and the repairs around the house."

"We'll need her address. How old is Anita?"

"It's 42 Willow Avenue, Saint Jude's. Gosh, now you're testing me. Around twenty-two or twenty-three I think... you know how time passes by so quickly."

"I do. Not that it matters. What about Sharon and Dylan? Do they live at the property?"

"No. They moved out."

"Oh? Why? Because they were older?"

He shrugged. "I guess. You know what some kids are like. They're eager to fly the nest as soon as they can afford it."

Kayli smiled considerately. The thought had crossed her mind when she was in her teens, not because she had fallen out with her parents. She loved them dearly, but she wanted to experience all that life had to offer at a young age. So she and her best friend, Lindy, had set up in a flat together. Everything had been going well until Lindy met Graeme Chance, a member of Kayli's team. They had fallen in love and decided to move in together soon after, leaving Kayli in the flat on her own. At first, she'd hated the solitude, but it didn't take her long to get used to it. Around that time, she'd decided to throw herself into work, and that was when her climb up the promotion ladder began. "Have you asked the children if they've heard from your brother?"

"Yes. None of them have. Poor Anita is distraught. She waited up all night for her father to come home. She was beside herself. She presumed her father had come back to my place on the Saturday night. I tried to reassure her. However, the doubt soon crept into my mind after a few hours. At the risk of repeating myself, this is unlike my brother to act this way, Inspector. I can feel it in my gut that something is wrong. I want to assure you that it is not my intention to waste police time. I'm adamant something has happened to my brother. I just need help proving that."

"We'll certainly do our best to help you, Mr. Potts. After what you've told me, that's the conclusion I have come to also."

He let out a relieved sigh and slouched back into his chair. "So, where do we go from here?"

"We'll question the children, see if they have any inclination as to where their father might have gone, and visit the flats to see first, if he turned up on Saturday night, and second, what time he left."

"I can't thank you enough for this, Inspector."

"We haven't found him yet. Mind you, if he doesn't want to be found, there really isn't a lot we can do about it."

He sat upright again and looked her in the eye. "I can honestly say that my brother has no reason on this earth why he should disappear. Not without telling one of us where he was going."

"I get that. However, in my experience, people put on a brave face when something is eating away at them inside. No one truly knows what another person is thinking deep down."

"I think you're wrong about that. My brother and I have always been extremely close. We contact each other daily, if only to say hello."

"Okay, you've convinced me. I'll keep you informed and ask that you do the same should your brother contact you or if something else puzzling you comes to light."

"I'll ring you immediately if that should happen."

Kayli withdrew a business card from her jacket pocket. "Ring me day or night." She slid the card across the table.

"Thank you. I'll keep it safe and ring you straight away. Is there anything else you need to know?"

Kayli turned to look at Donna. "Have we covered everything, Constable?"

"Not quite. Can you tell us what car your brother has and give us his registration number if you know it?"

Kayli smiled at Donna. "Excellent. Thanks for the reminder."

"He has a Ford Focus, a red one. I can't for the life of me remember the registration number, though. Can just about remember my own."

"No problem. We can retrieve that information from DVLA. Okay, leave it with us. We'll get started right away. I'll be in touch soon if we manage to find out anything."

He rose from his chair and stretched out a hand. "Thank you, Inspector. I look forward to hearing from you soon, with hopefully some positive news."

The three of them walked back to the reception area. Donna returned to the incident room while Kayli escorted Mr. Potts to the exit.

She turned to see the desk sergeant eagerly awaiting an update. "Nothing to report really, Ray. Mr. Potts seems adamant that his brother wouldn't just disappear like that, so we'll do our best to find out where he is and if anything untoward has happened to him."

"That's brilliant, ma'am. Thank you for taking the case on. I really appreciate it."

Kayli smiled and ran up the stairs. Waiting at the top was DCI Davis. "Hello, you. I came to see you. Dave said you were downstairs. Anything interesting?"

"Hello, ma'am. A missing persons case."

DCI Davis frowned. "Not your department, is it, Inspector?"

"Normally not. The desk sergeant said it was a friend of his, so I had a chat with him. I'm keen to find out what's happened to his brother. He's usually very reliable but hasn't been seen for a few days."

"Okay. I'd rather you not spend too many resources on this one, though, Inspector. Anyway, how is married life treating you? Before you answer that, I see by the twinkling in your eye that it's going well."

Kayli's cheeks warmed under the DCI's gaze. "Couldn't be happier, ma'am. Mark is still dealing with a few nightmares after his traumatic encounter, but he's getting there. He's at my dad's now, hopefully going over job prospects with him."

"That'll be good. He's not tempted to venture abroad again, I take it?"

"No. Although the money is good, it's just not worth the risk. He realises that now. We'll plod along on an insignificant inspector's salary for now," she added with a wry smile.

"If you're trying to wind me up, you've missed the mark. Women like me have fought hard to get you your salary. The least you can be is grateful for that."

Kayli laughed. "I thought I hadn't wound you up? Sounds like I succeeded to me."

"Anyway. I just wanted to drop by to welcome you back. Remember, my door is always open if you need to chat about anything in particular."

"You think I'm going to run out on you and put my life in danger again, don't you?"

DCI Davis turned and strode down the corridor towards her office and called over her shoulder, "The thought never even crossed my mind. I think you're far too intelligent to do that again."

Kayli laughed and headed back into the incident room without responding.

"I've got Mr. Potts's registration number," Donna called out as soon as Kayli entered the room.

"Excellent news. Can we start trawling through the CCTV footage around the location of the flats on Saturday around sixish and go from there? Dave, you and I will visit the flats to question the tenants, see what we can glean from them."

"I'm ready when you are," Dave replied, struggling to his feet. "Up, down, up, down," he muttered under his breath just loud enough for Kayli to hear.

"Would you rather I take Donna with me?"

"Ain't a partner allowed to complain now and again? I'll be fine once I'm moving. Any idea how many flats and floors we're going to have to tackle at the other end?"

Kayli smirked. "No idea, big man. Crikey, the sooner you get rid of those crutches, the better. Not sure I can take much more of your complaining."

He pulled a face and hobbled out of the incident room ahead, not bothering to hold the door open for her. Kayli glanced over her shoulder at Graeme and Donna. "Oops... do you think he's pissed off with me?"

Graeme and Donna sniggered.

"He'll be right once he's in the car, boss," Graeme said.

"I damn well hope so. Otherwise, I predict us having a very long day."

She followed her partner out of the room and rushed past him on the stairs. "Come on, slow coach. Get a wriggle on."

CHAPTER TWO

"Why are we doing things this way round?" Dave asked during the journey.

Kayli frowned. "Meaning what?"

"Isn't it normal for us to go and see the family first?"

"It is. I just thought I'd break the tradition. According to Samuel Potts, the last time he spoke to his brother was before Paul entered the flats he rents out."

"You thinking one of the tenants got a bit antsy and bumped him off?

"I'm really not sure what to think yet, without having spoken to anyone. Why don't we save this conversation for the return journey?"

"Okay, suits me. How's Mark coping with his injuries? It was a lovely service, by the way. Your face was a picture."

Kayli laughed. "The whole service was done and dusted before I could take a bloody breath. I was blown away. He's fine—getting there, anyway. Still having issues with the nightmares, though."

"Maybe he needs to have some form of counselling."

Kayli nodded. She'd thought about that suggestion herself over the past week. "Maybe you're right. He's in a buoyant mood at the moment. I'd hate to mess that up by suggesting he sees a shrink."

"I hear you. Getting back to work will be the making of him. I guarantee it."

"I do believe you're right, which is why he's visiting my dad today."

"Cool. Fingers crossed for him."

"Thanks. I think this is the house here." Kayli parked the car outside a three-storey Victorian detached house that seemed in reasonably good repair compared to its neighbours.

"Jesus, nice neighbourhood." Dave glanced up at the house then at the other houses surrounding them. "I bet we come back to your tyres being slashed."

Kayli punched his good leg. "Hey, don't say that. Maybe we should have called for backup. Think I'll ring Donna, tell her that if she doesn't hear from us within the next hour, to get uniform over here."

"I'd say half an hour if I were you. I bet the tenants aren't going to be the type to want a bloody conversation with us once they find out we're police."

Kayli placed the call. "Donna, it's me. Look, it's a pretty rough area. Just to be on the safe side, if you don't hear from us by ten thirty, I want you to get uniform over here."

"Got that. Leave it with me, ma'am. Be careful."

"We will. Dave can always protect us with his crutches." Kayli ended the call and smiled at her partner. "Right?"

"Not if I want to stay upright," he grumbled.

"Maybe I forgot about that part." Kayli laughed as they both got out of the car. She waited on the pavement and watched him struggle to his feet, knowing that if she attempted to help him, he would probably snap her head off.

Dave slammed the door shut behind him, and Kayli pressed the key fob to lock the doors then pressed it a second time to make sure. "Let's do this. Are you going to manage the steps up okay?"

"Yep, after you."

Kayli reached the top of the uneven steps and rang the first bell with the name of Hawkins on the intercom system.

"Yeah, what do you want?"

"Mr. Hawkins, I'm DI Kayli Bright. I'd like a word with you if I may?"

The intercom clicked, then there was silence.

"Guess he didn't want a word with you," Dave pointed out unnecessarily.

Kayli hit the same button on the intercom.

"Yeah, what do you want?"

"If you don't open the door, Mr. Hawkins, we'll break it down and haul you down the station to answer our questions. Am I making myself clear?"

The buzzer sounded. "Push the damn door."

Kayli pounced on the door before he changed his mind and locked it again. "At last. I get the impression he's not going to be happy to see us. I'll do the talking. You watch out and try to anticipate his actions."

"He wouldn't have the guts to hurt a police officer, surely."

They walked through the grubby hallway to the door at the end alongside the stairs. "Who knows? We're coming here blind, remember? No idea who these tenants are or what kind of record they've got."

"You're right. We should have brought backup with us."

"Too late now. We'll be fine. Just act tough." Kayli giggled.

Once Dave was settled into a comfortable position, leaning against the wall for added support in case he had to use his crutches to defend them, Kayli knocked on the door to the flat. Within seconds, a man in his early forties opened the door and glared at them. A large scar ran down the length of his right cheek.

"What's this about?"

Kayli flashed her warrant card in his face. "All right if we come in, Mr. Hawkins?"

"The place is a mess. Say what you've got to say here."

Kayli raised an eyebrow. "If you insist. When was the last time you saw your landlord, Paul Potts?"

He scratched the stubble on his chin. "I think it was Saturday. Why? Has he made some kind of complaint about me for my rent being late?"

"No. Can you tell me where you saw him?"

"What is this? Here, of course. I don't go out much."

"I take it he was chasing your back rent. Is that right?"

"Yeah. I told him I didn't have the money."

Kayli inclined her head. "Why don't you tell me how the conversation went?"

"What? You want it word for word? I've been asleep since then."

Kayli smiled tightly. "Do your best."

He tutted and leaned against the doorframe. "He wanted the rent, and I told him the Social were dragging their feet paying me. He told me he was giving me until the end of the week to find the money."

"Sounds reasonable enough to me."

"Maybe to you. Not to me, though. I can't come up with seven hundred quid at the drop of a hat."

"Ever thought of getting a job like normal folks?" She wouldn't normally be so judgemental, especially after her husband's own predicament, but the man's attitude was pissing her off.

He stood upright and pointed a finger. "Get off my case, lady. Any idea how hard it is for an ex-criminal to find a job around here?"

"I should imagine about as difficult as for anyone else. You said you don't go out much. Sorry, but a job isn't likely to come to your door, is it?"

"What gives you the right to come here and look down your nose at me like that?"

Kayli shook her head. "I wasn't aware that I was. I'm simply pointing out that there are dozens of jobs out there for those willing to get off their arses and find them, especially with bills to pay, such as rent."

"You have a smart mouth, bitch."

Dave shuffled forward slightly. "You might want to tone down your language, mate."

Hawkins looked Dave up and down and laughed. "Yeah, is that right. And who is going to make me?"

Kayli raised a hand between the two men. "This isn't getting us anywhere. What time did you see Mr. Potts on Saturday?"

"No idea. I didn't bother noting the time on my watch."

"How long was he here?"

"Long enough for me to tell him to come back at the end of the week and for him to warn me that if the rent wasn't forthcoming, he was going to kick me out."

"And what was your reaction to that?"

"I was livid. How would *you* react?"

Kayli shrugged. "Actually, I think it would spur me into action, and I'd be out there all hours, searching for a job instead of waiting for the Social to bail me out."

Hawkins's eyes narrowed. "As I've said already, how many employers do you know who are willing to take on an ex-con? It's hard, lady, damn hard."

"Do you have a probation officer?"

"Yeah, what of it?"

"That's part of their job, isn't it? To ensure you find a suitable job once you're out of prison."

"Maybe it used to be like that years ago, not nowadays."

"Too many ex-cons looking for too few jobs," Dave piped up.

"Ain't that the truth, man," Hawkins agreed. "Now, if you don't mind, my bacon buttie is getting cold."

"One last question before you get back to your breakfast. Do you know if Mr. Potts left after seeing you on Saturday?"

"Not sure. I heard raised voices upstairs a few minutes after he left my door. Might have been him. Don't quote me on that, though."

"Thanks, we'll look into that. Here's my card. If you think of anything else or if you hear something you think we might be interested in, will you ring me?"

"I might do." He slammed the door shut in their faces.

"Charming character," Kayli said as they moved away from Hawkins's door and started the climb up the stairs. "Are you all right?"

"I'm fine. Unfriendly bastard, wasn't he?"

"Just a tad. To be expected, I suppose." Kayli shuddered. "He gave me the creeps. Glad I brought you with me and not Donna."

"I got the impression he didn't like women much, as well. Bloody lazy bastard. There are dozens of jobs out there if these people took the time to look properly. Trouble is a lot of them don't like to get their hands dirty, so picking up litter or working on the bins is beneath most of them."

"That's so true. For the likes of him, anyway. Not sure it's the case for everyone on the dole though, mate. People with valued skills, for instance."

"Whatever. If you want things enough in this life, you'll get off your backside and get them."

"Okay, now you've put the world to rights, let's see what the rest of the tenants have to say." Kayli knocked on the next door they came to.

A young woman opened the door. She was holding a baby dressed in blue with jam around its face.

"Hi, sorry to trouble you. I'm DI Kayli Bright, and this is my partner, DS Dave Chaplin. Do you have a moment to chat?"

"About what? I'm busy tidying up after this little one."

"Sorry, we won't keep you long. I didn't catch your name."

"It's Colleen Porter. How can I help?"

"Maybe you can tell us when you last saw your landlord, Paul Potts?" Kayli asked with a glimmer of a smile.

"Not for a few weeks. Why?"

"We understand he was here on Saturday, chasing some of the tenants for rent that was due. You didn't happen to see him then?"

"No. Sorry. Is he in some kind of trouble?"

"Not that we know of. Did you hear any disturbance on Saturday evening?"

She frowned as she thought. "I really can't think of anything. Hey, but that doesn't mean a thing. I'm so preoccupied with this one most of the time, I don't have a clue what's going on around me."

"Not to worry. Thank you for your help. Oh wait, have you ever heard any of the other tenants having a go at Paul Potts or speaking badly about him perhaps?"

Colleen laughed. "You're kidding, right? Someone is always slagging him off about one thing or another around here."

"Do you live alone, Colleen?"

"Yes. Well, apart from this tyke, that is." She bounced the baby on her hip and smiled lovingly at him. The baby chortled and rubbed his jammy face against his mother's. "Damn, if you'll excuse me. I need to get this stuff off me before it goes hard."

"Thanks for your help. Can I leave a card? Ring me if you hear anything out of the ordinary regarding the other tenants."

"Not sure what that is supposed to mean, but yes, okay, I'll do that. Goodbye."

She closed the door, and Kayli and Dave shuffled along the landing to the next door.

Dave tapped on it with his crutch, but the door remained unanswered. "Bloody miracle. One of them is out there working for a change."

Kayli sniggered. "You're a harsh man, Dave Chaplin. Let's try the next one."

They moved a few feet, and Dave again knocked on the lower part of the grubby white door with the end of his crutch.

"Yeah, who is it?"

"Hi, I'm DI Bright. Can you open the door please?"

The door opened quickly to reveal a man with messy ginger hair. He had an e-cigarette hanging from his mouth. Kayli took his age to be around the mid-thirties mark. "Police? What can I do for you?"

"Sorry, I didn't catch your name, sir."

"Stuart Rawlinson."

"Hello there, Mr. Rawlinson. Can you tell us the last time you saw your landlord, Paul Potts?"

"Yep, on Saturday. He came looking for the rent. He was out of luck."

"Oh, why was that?"

"Because I didn't have it."

"And what was the outcome of that conversation, Mr. Rawlinson?"

"He told me to get it to him by the end of the week, or he'd kick me out."

"I should imagine a statement like that would make you angry, right?"

He hitched up his left shoulder. "I didn't think anything of it, to tell you the truth. Like the saying goes, you can't get blood out of a stone."

"Was this a regular occurrence, then?"

"Now and again, I'm a little tight on funds. Usually, he doesn't mind it. Maybe something else was pissing him off. He didn't seem his usual chatty self anyway."

"I see. Did you see him leave on Saturday?"

"Nope, can't say I did."

"Did you hear any raised voices, perhaps?"

He shook his head. "Nope, sorry. Anything else I can do for you nice people?"

"Nothing for now. Here's my card. If anything should come to mind, don't hesitate to ring me, day or night."

"Cheers. I'll do that. What's this all about anyway?"

"We're just trying to track Mr. Potts down. That's all."

His eyes widened, his interest sparked. "As in he's gone missing?"

"At the moment, yes. Let me know if you hear anything you think we should know about."

"I will. I take it this means he won't be back to collect the rent this week, then?"

"I'm sure he'll turn up soon enough, wanting his money, no doubt." Kayli smiled at the man as he shut the door. She turned to see Dave shaking his head. "What?"

"Are you telling me you didn't smell it?"

Kayli's brow furrowed. "Oh, the e-cigarette, you mean. Yep, wasn't keen on that smell at all."

"Except the smell wasn't coming from his fag. I smelt cannabis coming from inside the flat."

Kayli stared at the man's door. "You're kidding. Gosh, I've only had the misfortune to smell the stuff a few times. Still have problems detecting what drugs they are. I hope you don't recognise the smell from personal experience."

Dave puffed out his cheeks. "I refuse to answer that in case I incriminate myself."

Kayli's mouth gaped open for a moment before she said, "Bloody hell, when you think you know someone well, and they drop a bombshell on you like that."

Dave walked towards the next flight of stairs and mumbled. "It was in my youth. Get over it, boss."

She followed him slowly up the stairs. "You know what? I've never ever been tempted to do any kind of drugs. I'm shocked you went down that route, Dave. Does Suranne know?"

"No, and I'd really like to keep it that way if it's all the same to you."

"My lips are sealed. I'm shocked by your admission, though, I have to tell you."

"No shit, Sherlock," Dave replied, laughing.

They reached the third-floor landing, where there were two doors to choose from.

"This one looks as good a place as any to start." She knocked on the door.

It was a little while before it was answered by a very thin man who probably looked older than he actually was.

36

She held up her ID for him to check and introduced herself and Dave. "You are?"

"Michael Beech. What do you want? I haven't done anything against the law as far as I know."

"That's good to hear. We're making general enquiries at this point."

"Regarding what?" He fiddled with his spectacles, which had slipped on his nose.

"Can you tell me when you last saw your landlord, Mr. Potts?"

"A good few weeks ago. On rent day, I suppose it was. Why?"

"We've heard from some other tenants that he was at the property a few days ago, on Saturday. Are you telling me that you didn't see him then?"

He shook his head. "No, definitely not. Has something happened to him?"

"What makes you say that?"

"Well, not wishing to cast aspersions, but I heard raised voices here on Saturday evening." He looked over her shoulder at the door behind them.

"Out here?"

"Yep. I couldn't tell you if it was Paul shouting or Bob, to be honest."

"That's interesting. Thank you. I don't suppose you happened to hear what was being said?"

"No. I only heard the raised voices. You need to have a word with Bob about that."

"Thanks. Look, here's my card. Ring me if you hear anything that doesn't sit well with you."

"I don't understand. So are you saying that something has happened to Paul?"

"I'm not saying anything of the sort. Just ring me if you hear anything. Thanks very much."

"You're welcome. I think." He stepped back into his flat and closed the door.

"Okay, this is the last flat." Kayli walked the few steps to the next door, which was in need of a coat of fresh paint. She knocked, loosening some of the flaking paint, and wiped her hand down her trousers. "The place has become grubbier the higher we climb."

"I guess the term 'luxury penthouse suite' isn't common around these parts."

Kayli shook her head at her partner's attempt at a joke. She raised a hand to her lips and angled her ear towards the door. She thought she heard a door being opened and traffic noise. "Did you hear that?" she mouthed.

Dave nodded and whispered, "Knock again."

Kayli did just that, but the door remained firmly shut. "There was definitely movement inside." Kayli struck the door with her fist and shouted, "Bob, open up. I know you're in there. It's the police."

Nothing. The door remained closed.

Kayli bolted down the stairs two at a time.

"Stop! Wait for me," Dave called out behind her.

"I can't. He's getting away. Stop there and call Donna. Get backup here right away."

"Be careful. Don't go doing anything rash."

"I won't. Trust me," Kayli called, running out the front door and onto the street. She surveyed the area from the steps then descended them and ran around to the back of the house, down the side alley. Looking up, she saw an emergency escape route from the third floor, a set of metal stairs. She ran the length of the alley but found nothing. Smashing her fist against her thigh, she shouted, "Damn. He's gone."

Looking up the alley, she saw her partner coming towards her. "Anything? Did you see him?"

"No. He was long gone before I got here. Well, if that doesn't reek of guilt, I don't know what does. I'm going back to the house. I need to find out his full name before we can start tracing him. Why don't you sit in the car, Dave? You've got quite a sweat on you." She handed him her keys and trotted up the alley ahead of him.

At the top of the steps, she jotted down all the names alongside the buzzers. "Okay, Mr. Bob Nuttall, let's see what we can dig up about you and see why you took off the way you did."

Dave was trying to navigate his access to the car when she arrived. "Need a hand?"

"Nope, I'm fine." He collapsed into the passenger seat and dragged the crutches into the car beside him. "Did you get his name?"

"Yep. Bob Nuttall. I jotted down all the other names too. Let's run background checks on all of them. It can't hurt. Maybe something else will show up that will help to solve the case. We're going to have to wait here until uniform arrive." She pricked her ear up in the air when she heard a distant siren. "Sounds like they're on their way. Damn, I didn't even think about there being a possible fire escape to the house. I must be losing my touch."

"It's the law, I think you'll find. Don't beat yourself up. We'll catch up with the bastard soon enough. He's running for a reason. We just need to find out what that reason is. Here are our boys now."

"I'll just have a quick word, leave them to carry out a search of the area. We won't be able to search his flat until we get a warrant. Then we'll shoot back to the station."

A patrol vehicle pulled up alongside her. She flashed her ID at the two uniformed officers as they got out of the car and apprised them of the situation.

"I'll call for K9 assistance, ma'am," the younger officer said.

"Good idea. Let me know how you get on. The suspect's name is Bob Nuttall." Kayli joined Dave at the car. "I hope they find him. At the moment, he's got to be our main suspect."

CHAPTER THREE

"Donna, I need you and Dave to work together on this one. Go through the list of names. I want everything you can find on these guys, including where they take a piss and who they shag. Obviously, I need you to begin with Bob Nuttall. The sooner we can find him and bring him in for questioning, the better."

Donna nodded, jotted down half the names on a sheet of paper and handed it to Dave. "On it now, boss."

"Any luck on the car yet, Graeme?"

He didn't look up from the screen, just shook his head. "Nothing yet."

"Let me know right away when you trace it. Okay, I can't sit around here on my hands. I'm going to visit the children, starting with Anita Potts."

"Alone?" Dave looked at her, surprised.

"Yes, I'll be fine. You're better off here, Dave. That has nothing to do with the fact that your leg is hindering you at the moment, either. The more people we have checking out the backgrounds, the better, for obvious reasons."

"Okay, if you're sure. Can you check in before and after you enter the house?"

Kayli chortled. "I'll be fine." She extracted a small canister from her pocket and waved it at him. "I have this with me for peace of mind. However, you're forgetting who I tangled with last month and who came out on top."

Dave tutted. "No, I'm not. You also had half a dozen shit-hot soldiers working alongside you."

"Not quite. Four soldiers plus my brother," she replied, pulling a face at him. "If it will make you any happier, I will check in all the same. See you later."

Kayli left the station, and twenty minutes later, she pulled up outside a smartly presented, white-rendered detached house with bright-red woodwork around the doors and the windows. It was a sharp contrast to the condition of the flats she had visited earlier. The small garden on either side of the path consisted of a narrow flower bed around a piece of lawn that was cut short, despite the time of year. It was clear that someone cherished the home and its garden. She recalled what Paul Potts's brother had said about him caring for the garden.

She rang the bell and turned to survey the neighbourhood. There wasn't a grubby house or garden in sight. She couldn't determine whether the neighbours were in competition with each other or simply proud of their community. On a nearby lamppost, Kayli spotted a yellow Neighbourhood Watch sign.

"A caring community, such a rarity nowadays," she muttered.

She heard the chain being removed from the door before it was opened by a blonde, frail-looking young lady who was wearing large-framed spectacles and had freckles on her makeup-free face. "Hello, can I help?" she asked, her voice weak and fearful.

Kayli smiled warmly and flashed her ID. "Are you Anita?"

The young woman nodded.

"I'm DI Kayli Bright. Your uncle Samuel came to see me regarding your father. Would it be possible to come in and have a chat with you?"

She stood behind the door, allowed Kayli to enter the property then closed the door quietly behind her. Kayli followed her through a narrow carpeted hallway to a small kitchen at the rear.

"I was just about to make a pot of tea. Would you like one?"

"Is it possible to have a coffee instead? Instant will do, of course."

"Please, take a seat." Anita pointed at the small kitchen table against the wall.

Kayli pulled out a chair and withdrew her notebook from her pocket before she sat down. "I take it you haven't heard from your father in the last few hours?"

"No, nothing. I'm struggling to cope with his disappearance, if you must know. That's why my uncle agreed to call at the station. I keep breaking down in tears every time I think of what my father must be going through." She removed her glasses and reached for a tissue to wipe away her tears.

"Please, try and stay positive. We're doing our very best to find your father. I'm sure it's only a matter of time before that happens. Are you up to answering a few questions? We'll take it slowly, at your own speed. I'll completely understand if it gets too much for you and you want to stop. I promise."

Anita finished preparing the drinks and joined Kayli at the table. Her hands shook when she deposited the two mugs on the table, spilling some of the contents. Kayli knew she would have to be patient and tread carefully with the woman if she was going to get any sense out of her.

"I'm not sure I can tell you much, Inspector."

"When was the last time you saw your father?"

Her head bowed, and she stared at the contents of her mug, her hands clasped tightly around the china. "It must have been five on Saturday."

Kayli jotted down the young woman's answers. "Where was that?"

"Here. Dad had just finished watching the football results on BBC, then he suddenly announced he was going out. I was halfway through making the dinner at the time. We usually eat around sixish. I tried to object, but he's too obstinate and set in his ways to listen to me. He told me to leave his meal in the oven or put it in the microwave for when he returned."

"Did your father say where he was going?"

"Yes, to pick up the rent due to him from the flats we own."

Kayli looked up to find Anita was still staring at the mug. "Can you tell me what sort of mood he was in?"

"He was pretty narked that Bristol City had lost their match before he left. Don't ask me who they were playing. I have no interest in the sport."

Kayli smiled. "Likewise. Did your father leave here angry, then? Is that what you're telling me?"

Anita looked up. "Not sure *angry* is the right word. More pissed off, I'd say."

"How often does your father visit the flats?"

"More often than he should. His friend has a few rental houses, and he never has to badger the tenants to hand over their money. They always pay by direct debit, but then all his tenants work for a living and aren't reliant on the Social for their money."

Kayli noticed a bit more fight in Anita when she mentioned the tenants. "Has he had a lot of problems with the tenants in the past?"

"Dad took over the house about a year ago. Bought it with the insurance money after Mum died. It's been like an albatross around his neck ever since. The people down there can't understand that they have to pay their way in this world. All of them think that society owes them something. They need to get off their backsides and find a bloody job."

"Have you met the tenants, Anita?"

Her head shook fiercely. "No. Dad refused to let me go down there with him. He thought the tenants were too dangerous for me to have anything to do with them."

"How strange. I was down there this morning, and to be honest, I didn't really get that impression."

She looked Kayli in the eye. "But you're the police. Wouldn't they treat you differently to someone they owed money to?"

Kayli shrugged. "Perhaps you're right about that. Has your father ever been attacked by any of the tenants?"

Anita's gaze dropped down to the table again. "He's had a few run-ins with a couple of them. One or two roughed him up a little. You know, pushed him or jabbed him in the chest once or twice to intimidate him, but nothing more than that, really."

"Okay, that's still something that should never happen. Can you give me their names?"

She swallowed noisily before she answered. "One of them was Nigel Hawkins, and the other was the bloke on the top floor, Bob Nuttall."

"Any idea when the hassle took place? Was it recently?"

"A few weeks ago with Bob. The argument with Nigel, on the other hand, took place a few months ago. I pleaded with him to kick them out. We have a list of people who have contacted us, wanting a flat. I begged Dad to give them a chance. He always said it was far more hassle than it was worth to keep changing tenants. I suppose he was right. It *is* a lot of trouble. However, my take on it is that it would be far less bother for Dad to have to contend with. Buying the house was supposed to secure his future, give him a reasonable pension to live on, not create more bloody work for him. He's under the doctor for high blood pressure, you know. All because of that damn place. It's just not worth all the aggro. Now this…"

Kayli sensed that Anita was working herself up into a frenzy and covered her hand with hers. "Please, try not to upset yourself. We'll get to the bottom of this. I'm sorry, but I have to ask. Is there any possibility your father might have ended his own life?"

She shook her head adamantly. "No, there is no way on this earth he'd do such a thing. He was really down last year when we lost Mum, which is only natural, I suppose, but we pulled together and came through that tough time. He relies on me as much as I rely on him. He is open with me, Inspector, very honest with his feelings, unlike other men I know. If he had dark thoughts along those lines, I'm sure he wouldn't hesitate to confide in me."

"Okay, sorry. I had to ask. At least we can discount that route from our enquiry. And you don't think it was possible for him to take off on a break of sorts without telling you?"

"Absolutely not. Why would he arrange to meet my uncle down the pub on Saturday evening if he intended to go away? I truly believe that something bad has happened to him, Inspector."

"Yes, your uncle mentioned they had agreed to meet and that he was in regular contact with his brother."

"Every day. They're very close. Closer still since my grand-parents died around ten years ago."

"I'm sorry to hear that. Was it an accident? Did they die together?"

"Yes, they broke through the central reservation on the M5 and caused a multiple pile-up on the opposite side of the motorway. We were all devastated at the time. Granddad was in his seventies but had always been a truly safe driver, never going above the speed limit, even when he overtook another vehicle."

"So sorry to hear that. Was the incident investigated?"

"Yes. They discovered that something had gone wrong with the car's brake system. I don't know the ins and outs, Inspector. I just know that we were all very traumatised at the time. Of course, back then, Dad had Mum around for support. Not sure how he would have coped if she hadn't still been with us. Since then, Dad and Uncle Samuel have been inseparable."

"I see. That's very sad. Sorry for your loss. Your uncle mentioned that you have a brother and a sister. Am I right?"

"Technically, they're my half-brother and half-sister, although we were brought up together. My dad married their mum twenty-five years ago after their own father ran out on them. It took a while for our mum to track their father down to enable her to divorce him so that she could marry my dad, but eventually, things turned out for the best."

"And you're all close now?"

"Yes, Sharon was here yesterday, comforting me. My step-brother, Dylan, was doing a shift at the pub where he works. They share a house together."

"What does Dylan do there?"

"He flits between the bar and serving tables, even helps out in the kitchen sometimes when they are short-handed. I suppose you'd call him an all-rounder."

"The name of the pub?"

"The Old Swan in the town centre."

Kayli had a vague recollection where the pub was situated, and she noted down the name. "And what about Sharon? Where does she work?"

"She's a carer in a care home. The Nightingale Care Home."

"Thanks. I'll need to speak to them both to see if they have seen your father since Saturday."

"They haven't. Sharon called round, and I rang Dylan. To be honest, they usually come round most Sundays. I generally cook a family roast dinner. I couldn't face doing that yesterday. Sharon ended up going out to fetch a KFC instead, not that I ate much of it. She ate most of mine and took the rest home for Dylan."

"What's their take on your father's disappearance?"

"They just think he's taken off somewhere to spend some time alone. They're wrong, though. They don't know my father like I know him. He wouldn't go off without telling either Uncle Samuel or me where he was going."

"I have my team searching the area for your father's car. I'm sure the cameras will highlight it soon around the city. I have every confidence once we locate it, the mystery of where your father is will be solved. In the meantime, I suggest you stay either near or in the house at all times in case he returns."

"I will. I rang my firm today and called in sick. Told them I wouldn't be back until the end of the week."

"What do you do for a living, Anita?"

"I'm a secretary at an estate agent's in town. They weren't too happy with me, but that's tough. I need to be here for when he comes home. If he comes home…"

"Is there anything else you can tell me about your father? Perhaps he's fallen out with someone lately?"

Anita looked up, thought over the question then shook her head. "Not that I can recall. Dad is pretty easy-going most of the time. It's just that mob at the flats that rile him now and again."

"Does your father have any other family in the area?"

"No. There's only Samuel and him now. All our extended family are no longer with us."

"Is Samuel married?"

"Yes, to Dorothy. They have a son and daughter, Alan and Jill Potts."

"Do you have their details for me? An address is preferable."

Anita pushed back her chair and left the room. She returned, carrying her handbag and a small address book in her right hand. "Yes, here we are. I don't really have much to do with them now that Nan and Granddad are no longer with us. It's sad when family members drift apart." She offered Kayli the address book.

Kayli wrote down the names and addresses and handed the book back to Anita. "Thanks. I'll pay them a visit, if only to put my mind at rest that I've covered all the angles."

"That's all I can tell you, really, Inspector. Please, I'm begging you not to discount this case in favour of another one that you might deem more important. I honestly feel it in my stomach something terrible has occurred and that my father is in desperate need of our help… if he's still alive, that is." Fresh tears welled up in her eyes.

"Please don't upset yourself. If your father wants to be found, I promise you that we'll find him. However, if he's determined not to be found, then it is totally out of our hands. I'll register him as a missing person when I return to the station. I'm sure we'll find out where he is soon. Just stay positive."

Anita walked towards the front door of the house and opened it. "Have you ever been parted from a loved one, Inspector?"

Kayli smiled and nodded. "As it happens, yes, I have. Recently, in fact. Why do you ask?"

"Then you'll know the empty feeling I have buried deep inside at present. It's a terrible sensation and one that I am keen to get rid of. Please, please, do your best to bring my father home to me. I'm lost without him. He's my absolute world. I could never forgive myself if I found out that something bad has happened to him."

Kayli patted Anita on the forearm. "Honestly, you have my word. My team are the best in the area. If we can't find him, then no one will. Rest assured we won't stop the investigation until we have the answers that we are seeking."

"Thank you. I believe you and wish you luck in your endeavours."

Kayli handed Anita a business card. "If anything should come to mind, don't hesitate to ring me, day or night. I'll try and keep you updated as the case progresses, but give me and my team time to get the investigation underway first. We need something concrete to go on before we can be optimistic about bringing your father back to you."

"You're a good person, Inspector. I can tell that by the gentle manner you have."

Kayli winked. "Just don't tell my team what a soft touch I am. I'd never get any work out of them if they discovered that. Look after yourself and keep your strength up."

"I'll do my best. It was lovely to meet you. I feel confident the right person is in charge of my father's case and his destiny."

"Speak soon." Kayli left the house and jumped back in the car. She checked in with Dave and then had a sudden need to ring Mark. She dialled his mobile and put it on speakerphone while she drove back to the station. "Hello, you. How's it going?"

"Kayli, I'm going to have to ring you back. I'm en route to a job interview at present. I need to keep my head clear, if that's all right?"

"That's wonderful news. Give me a call later to tell me how you got on. Good luck. I love you."

"Thanks. I love you too," Mark said, sounding a little distracted.

Kayli ended the call with mixed feelings, wondering if he was being deliberately evasive about what job he was being interviewed for. The thought crossed her mind to ring her father, but she stopped herself. Mark would have a fit if she went behind his back to find out. She would just have to wait and see what the outcome of the interview was when she got home that evening.

She drove back to the station on autopilot then walked through the reception area and up the stairs to the incident room without seeing or acknowledging any of her colleagues, which was unusual for her. When she arrived, she found Donna standing at the whiteboard, noting down the information they had gathered so far on the case.

"Hi. Are you okay, boss?" Dave asked as she swept past him in a daze.

"Huh? Sorry, yes. All is well with me. What have you managed to find out in my absence?"

Donna smiled at her then pointed at the names she had written on the board. "Our main man, Bob Nuttall, is thirty-five. He's been in and out of prison since his early twenties."

"For what?" Kayli asked, perching on the desk beside her.

"Mainly stealing cars, some of which were used in subsequent robberies. Others, he sold on to unsuspecting garages. And the biggie is that he was charged with aggravated assault on a police officer who was trying to arrest him."

Kayli's eyes narrowed. "The nasty piece of shit. That snippet alone makes me even more determined to find him. Any news from the uniformed officers at the scene on that, Dave?"

Her partner shook his head. "Not heard anything yet. Do you want me to chase it up?"

"Let's give them half an hour then ring them. Damn, why didn't I realise there was a bloody fire escape he could use?"

"You can't blame yourself," Dave said.

"Easier said than done. You know what a perfectionist I am."

"Yeah, I think we all know that by now. To the point of being anal about it. Give yourself a break. We'll find the bastard soon enough."

Kayli turned sharply to look at him. "Anal? Did you really say that about me?"

Dave's cheeks coloured up under her scrutinising glare. "A figure of speech," he replied uncertainly.

Kayli's smile made him let out a relieved breath. "You can be so gullible at times." Turning back to Donna, she said, "Okay, I'm glad you put him at the top of the suspect list. I think we're onto something with him. Why else would he run? What have you got on the others?"

"We have Nigel Hawkins, aged forty. Also spent most of his time in and out of prison on relatively minor offences, which include an attempted robbery at a small supermarket and ABH on a bouncer a few years ago."

"Nice to know that the rehabilitation these guys receive inside is working… not! More taxpayers' money wasted by the system. Don't get me started on that topic, for God's sake. Next one, Donna?"

Donna pointed at the third name she had written on the board. "Stuart Rawlinson. He's fifty, mostly banged up for pickpocketing, seen as being more of an opportunist rather than a hardened criminal, I guess."

"He didn't really strike me as being a man capable of harming anyone else, if I'm honest. Next?"

"Michael Beech. He's forty-three. He's been inside for minor crimes over the years, such as shoplifting. On one occasion, he nicked a complete woman's outfit, including all the underwear, from a major store on the high street."

"Not Marks and Spencer's?"

Donna nodded.

"At least he has good taste in underwear. That's where I buy most of my stuff."

Dave cleared his throat. "Umm… too much information, boss. Not sure I'll be able to shift the image you've just conjured up in my mind now."

Kayli rolled her eyes at Donna. "Let's ignore him. Anything else? There are six flats at the house. One of those was inhabited by a young woman with a baby, Colleen Porter, if I remember rightly. Do we know who lives in the other flat?"

"I'm aware of Colleen. Do you want me to add her to the list?"

"Might as well, Donna."

The constable added the name and put a ring around it like she had to the others on the board. "She has no significant other. Lives alone with the child on welfare."

"Any prior record?"

"Nothing of interest. She was arrested for being abusive to an officer whilst she was drunk, but the charges were later dropped."

"Fair enough. That leaves just the one flat unaccounted for."

"I have the name Lee Russell. His record goes back a while. He was found guilty of robbing a warehouse. Since then, he's kept his nose clean."

"Good job, Donna. It makes things a whole lot clearer from the outset. Can you do me a favour and start delving into the family's background now? Anita Potts is Paul's daughter. There are two stepchildren, as well, Sharon and Dylan Potts. They took on his name when Anita and Paul got married. I haven't had the privilege of meeting either of them yet, but Anita was beside herself earlier when I called at the house."

"On it now, boss." Donna marched back to her desk and began tapping at the keys on her keyboard.

Kayli's mobile rang. She answered it on the second ring. "DI Bright."

"Hello, ma'am. This is Constable Lockard. We met earlier. Just wanted to inform you that we've had no luck at the scene. Even the dog didn't pick up a scent. The K9 officer said if that was the case, it usually means the suspect escaped from the area in a vehicle."

"Damn! Thanks for letting me know." Kayli ended the call. "No sign of Nuttall at the scene. Dave, do me a favour and get on to DVLA. See what car he drives, then issue an alert for it."

"Will do. Will it be worth calling on the media for help?"

Kayli chewed her lip. "I know he's on the run, but that doesn't mean that he's guilty of anything yet. For all we know, he could owe a loan shark money, and that's who he thought was at his door." She threw her arms up in the air and pushed herself off the desk. "I don't know. I'm just playing devil's advocate there. I think we'll play it cool for now, try and trace his car and him, then go from there. Agreed?"

"Agreed. I'll let you know when I've got the information to hand."

Kayli walked over to Graeme. "Any news on the CCTV or the ANPRs for Potts's car?"

"Nothing yet. That area is super busy with vehicles."

"Stick with it, Graeme. Let me know as soon as you have anything. I'll be in my office, guys." Kayli stopped off at the vending machine to get her regular fix of caffeine then sat at her desk, weeding through her paperwork for the next hour or so until Dave knocked on her door. "Come in. What have you found? Anything?"

Dave hobbled towards the chair and dropped into it. "I managed to trace Nuttall's car. Can't imagine he'll get very far. He drives an old car. An Opel Manta. Not many of those around nowadays, I can tell you."

"That's great news. It should mean he'll be easy to track down then, right?"

Dave hitched up a shoulder. "You'd think so, unless he hides out somewhere and places the car in a garage."

Kayli pulled a face. "Not sure that's a likely scenario, Dave. Have you circulated the details?"

"Yep, just done it. Is there anything else you want me to do?"

Kayli looked at her watch. It was almost five thirty. "I think we've done enough for one day between us. I say we wrap things up and get ready to leave at six."

"Fine by me. Do you want to start early in the morning?"

"Let's get here around eight thirty. Ask the team if they concur. Thank them all for their effort today. I'll just work my way through the rest of this crap and be on my way."

"See you tomorrow, then." Dave leaned on his crutches to stand up.

"Have a good evening."

"You too."

After completing her paperwork, Kayli walked through the deserted office, switched off the lights for the evening and left the station. She rang Mark's mobile before she pulled out of the car park. "Hi, only me. I'm on my way home now. We discussed getting a takeaway this morning. Any idea what you fancy? Chinese or Indian?"

"Nothing. Dinner is all in hand. I picked something up on the way home. Just get home soon. I miss you."

Her heart melted. "I'll be twenty minutes. How did the interview go?"

"Impatient, as always. I'll let you know when you get home."

"All right. See you soon."

Kayli placed her mobile on the passenger seat and selected first gear. The traffic was dying down at this time of night, thankfully, an added bonus for deciding to delay her departure. She couldn't wait to see Mark again.

She parked the car outside their two-bed terraced house and rushed up the path. Entering the house, she slipped off her shoes in the hallway before making her way through the lounge and into the kitchen. "Wow! What's all this?"

The table was laid with a deep-red tablecloth, and two glasses of red wine adorned two place settings. In the middle of the table was a huge bunch of bright-coloured flowers.

Mark walked towards her, his arms outstretched, ready for her to step into. "I thought I'd spoil my princess for a change. You always look after me so well. I'm just repaying the compliment."

"You shouldn't have. I don't expect this from you, Mark."

"I know you don't. I'm glad you're surprised." He kissed her then pulled out a chair at the table. "Would madam care to take a seat? Dinner will be a few more minutes. Enjoy a glass of wine while you wait."

"Blimey, a girl could get used to this. Dinner smells divine. What are we having?"

"Nothing too fancy. A nice piece of steak I picked up from the butcher's down the road. He gave me strict instructions on how to cook it so I didn't mess it up. By the looks of things, I think I've done a grand job. Oops, I better get back to it before I tempt fate."

"You're the best, Mark. I wasn't expecting this. It's such a lovely surprise to come home to."

"Good. Life should all be about surprising the ones you love now and again. We have a lot to be thankful for, right?"

She smiled lovingly at him. "We do indeed. You haven't told me how the interview went."

"Ssh... let's eat dinner first."

She narrowed her eyes as she watched him turn the steak in the pan and press it down with his fork. He then opened the oven, removed the pan of chips and set it on the top of the stove. He expertly plated up the meal under her watchful gaze. She felt so proud of him. He'd never even knocked up an omelette for her in the past, let alone attempted a proper dinner—a steak dinner, at that.

He deposited the plate in front of her and kissed her cheek. "I hope it tastes as good as it looks. Enjoy."

"It looks and smells wonderful."

"Fillet steak with a creamy mustard sauce, oven chips, peas, mushrooms and tomatoes, m'lady."

"Gosh, maybe you should take over cooking the meals. It's a darn sight better than anything I could tempt you with."

His gaze dropped to the table.

"Mark? What is it?"

He lifted his head and smiled warmly. "Just eat your meal before it gets cold. We'll talk afterwards. How was your day at work?"

Hmm... a swift change of subject. What the hell is going on? Rather than put a dampener on the evening, she decided to play along with him. "Tricky case we've taken on, but then, aren't they all to begin with?"

"I have every confidence in you and your team uncovering the facts. What is it? A murder case?"

She swallowed the piece of succulent steak before she replied. "No. It's a missing persons case at present. However, we have a list of suspects who all have extremely dodgy pasts, and one of them is on the run, which has obviously raised our suspicions."

"Daft thing to do. I wouldn't want a ballsy character like you on my tail. That's for sure. The idiot has no idea what he's let himself in for. I hope you catch him soon. I take it the runner is a male?"

"He is. We've put an alert out on his car." She sipped her wine. "This is scrummy. You can definitely cook this again."

"I don't mind doing it on special occasions, if you let me."

"You won't get any arguments from me." They ate the rest of the meal in a satisfied silence, each of them savouring the quality of the meat.

Once they had finished, Mark ordered Kayli to stay put. He removed the plates and walked over to the fridge, where he extracted two tall glasses. Kayli tried to work out what the dessert was but failed.

"What is it?" she asked, peering into the glass.

"Summer fruit fool." He smiled triumphantly. "Yeah, I know, but it's the middle of winter. The butcher had a packet of summer fruits in his freezer and threw them in free of charge. He told me to add either cream or natural yoghurt, and voila! This is the result."

"You never cease to amaze me. What did you go for in the end? Cream or yoghurt?" She dipped her spoon in and tasted a mouthful. "Cream, right? Bang goes my diet for the day."

Mark tutted. "You're still too skinny anyway. You could do with fattening up a little. Yes, it's cream. Is it good?"

"Scrummy. Hey, you'll be entering *MasterChef* on the TV soon if you keep this up."

"Hardly. I'll definitely take that as a compliment, though. Eat up."

They finished their dessert, then Kayli insisted she should do the washing up while Mark put his feet up in the lounge. During her chores, she rehearsed how she should broach the subject again about his interview. The last thing she wanted to do was to put a dampener on the perfect evening.

She heard him laughing at a programme on Sky as she cleared the last of the dishes away. Taking her glass of wine and the rest of the bottle, she walked into the lounge and slipped onto the sofa beside him. Mark flung an arm around her shoulder and continued to laugh at the comedy show. Kayli felt nervous, eager to find out what was going on, but too worried to raise the subject. They sat like that until the show ended. Then she reached for the control and switched off the TV.

"Hey, I was watching that."

Kayli shook her head. "I need to hear how you got on today, Mark. Don't keep me in suspense any longer."

He tried to tug her against him for a cuddle, but she pulled back and remained upright. "All right. God, you can be such a stubborn..."

"You were about to say?"

"Stubborn mule. Although yes, I was tempted to call you something far worse."

"Sticks and stones, matey. Get on with it."

He took a sip of his wine, yet another form of delay. Kayli took the glass from his hand and placed it on the coffee table in front of them. "Speak."

He swept a hand over his face. "You'll be pleased to know that I got the job. That means I can contribute to the household expenses once again."

She nodded slowly. "Okay, that's good. Now tell me what the job is. Why are you being so evasive, Mark? I'm not going to like this, am I?"

"I'm not sure." He inhaled a deep breath.

Kayli swiped at his chest. "Tell me," she ordered through gritted teeth, her patience finally snapping.

He looked ahead of him and announced, "I'm going to be a bouncer at the nightclub in town."

Her heart sank. "Oh crap! You're kidding me!"

"Nope. It's a temporary measure until something more suitable comes along. Anyway, don't blame me. Blame your dad. He's the one who put my name forward."

"Don't worry. I'll be having a quiet word in his ear. This means that we'll never see each other. We'll be working opposite shifts."

"Bear with me, Kayli. You know what they say: it's far better to get employment if you're already employed."

Kayli collapsed against his chest. "I know. We'll both scour the job-vacant ads to find something more suitable. Bloody hell, a bouncer. At the club in town, the StarGazer?"

"That's the one."

"Jesus, we get more calls about that place than any other establishment in town. It attracts trouble like a bloody magnet. Did they say why they have a vacancy?"

"The previous bouncer moved on. That's all the manager would tell me. I'm sorry, love. It's not the best start to married life. Look at it this way—at least I won't be under your feet all the time around here."

Kayli sat upright. "I think I'd prefer it if you *were* under my feet."

He pulled her close and kissed the top of her head. "You know you don't mean that. Let's give it a chance. A month at the most. If we both feel the same after that, I'll jack it in. How's that?"

"Okay, that's fair enough."

The topic was forgotten after that, and they spent the rest of the evening snuggled up on the sofa, sipping their wine.

CHAPTER FOUR

Dave was the last member of the team to arrive, and he looked knackered before his day had even started.

"Everything all right, Dave?" Kayli asked.

"Sleepless night, that's all. Have you ever tried sleeping in the same position with a leaded weight on your leg?"

Kayli cringed. "Nope, can't say I have. Soon be over with, eh?"

"Not soon enough," he grumbled.

Kayli knew his foul mood would disintegrate as soon as caffeine penetrated his system. She bought a coffee and deposited it on his desk on her way to the whiteboard.

"You're too generous. Thank you. What's on the agenda for today?"

"To start with, I think we need to go over old ground to see if we've missed anything."

After recapping where the investigation had taken them the day before, Dave suggested, "We still need to pay the stepkids a visit."

Kayli tilted her head. "You're right. Any specific reason you raised that point?"

Dave shrugged. "Maybe they might be able to tell us something that Anita couldn't."

"Such as?"

Dave widened his eyes. "I don't know. Perhaps Paul Potts shielded Anita from something and possibly confided in Sharon or Dylan."

Kayli nodded. "Hmm... you might have something there. Donna, can you jot down their address for me? Dave and I will trundle out there after the rush-hour traffic has died down."

"And what if they're at work?" Dave replied.

"Then we'll visit them there. Anita gave me the information about both of their workplaces. Donna, did you manage to squeeze in doing the background checks on the family?"

"I did. Nothing of interest has shown up at all. Sorry, boss."

"Not your fault. Okay, so that leaves the CCTV footage and the ANPR images. Graeme, anything yet?"

Looking defeated, he shook his head. "It's so busy in that area. I'm not trying to make excuses. I'll get back to it now."

"I appreciate how difficult it is. Do you need a hand sifting through the images?"

"No, I'll be fine. I have another angle I want to try today. I'll do that and get back to you."

"Good man. Okay, give me ten minutes to look through the post, then we'll make tracks, Dave."

Kayli walked into her office. She sat down at her desk and tackled the three brown envelopes sitting there. They contained two updated procedures from head office that she had already implemented with the team and a note referring to a case she'd solved before her overseas adventure. She dealt with the final letter then left her office again. "Are you ready, Dave?"

"That was quick. Haven't even finished my cuppa yet."

"Take it with you. I want to get cracking on this."

"Thought you were going to let the traffic die down a bit before venturing out."

"It's a woman's prerogative to change her mind. Sup up."

Dave gulped down his lukewarm coffee and hoisted himself to his feet.

"We'll be a couple of hours. Keep digging, guys. If you stumble across anything interesting, ring me immediately."

~ ~ ~

Kayli drew up outside Sharon and Dylan's house. It was a small terraced house not dissimilar in style to the one she lived in. "Do you want to stay here while I check to see if anyone is at home?"

"Thanks. That would be great."

Kayli left the car and walked up the cracked concrete path. In the front garden, litter was scattered across both sides of the lawn, which was overgrown. She rang the bell and looked up at the bedroom window. A second later, the curtain twitched slightly. A woman wearing a pink towelling robe opened the door. Kayli could tell she had just woken by the amount of sleepiness surrounding her eyes.

She flashed her ID. "DI Kayli Bright. Sorry to disturb you. Are you Sharon Potts?"

The woman scratched her head and frowned. "Yes. What's this about?"

"Perhaps it would be better if we came inside to speak."

"We?"

Kayli motioned for Dave to join her. "Yes, my partner is in the car."

"If you have to. I must warn you, though, I was on the night shift last night. I only dropped off to sleep around eight."

Kayli felt the guilt poke her. "I'm really sorry. We shouldn't keep you too long. Here's Dave now."

Dave came to a halt beside her. "DS Dave Chaplin, ma'am."

"Hello," Sharon said, stepping back behind the door and holding her robe tightly at her chest. "Go through to the first room on the left. Excuse the mess if there is any. My brother can be a mucky bugger at times."

Once in the room, Sharon invited them to take a seat on the sofa while she switched on the gas fire to take the chill off the room and sat in the armchair opposite them. "How can I help?" Sharon asked, the frown still prominent on her brow.

"Is your brother home at present?"

"No. He works very long hours at the pub. They take the piss, if you must know. There was a delivery coming in early this morning, and the owner had a meeting with his accountant that he couldn't postpone."

"Never mind. We can catch up with him later. Tell me, have you spoken to Anita recently?"

Sharon's frown deepened. "Yesterday, I did. Why?" She gasped. "Oh no, has something happened to her?"

"Not as far as we know. I was there yesterday, getting some background information into your stepfather's disappearance. I take it you haven't heard from him in the last few days? Since he went missing?"

Sharon looked down at the carpet by her feet. "No. It's just dreadful to think he might be out there somewhere, needing our help. Have you been to the flats, to question the tenants?"

"Is there a specific reason why you should ask that?"

"Not really. Just that they aren't the friendliest of characters, and some of them owed Paul a lot of money in rent. He was livid about that. Actually, he was worse than that, really angry. That was the last time anybody heard from him, when he went there on Saturday to ask the ones who owed him money to cough up. Funny that he should go missing either during that visit or sometime afterwards. I know who I would be questioning if I were in your shoes."

Kayli smiled to reassure the woman. "We were there yesterday. We spoke to all the tenants, bar one."

Sharon looked up and narrowed her eyes. "Go on, surprise me."

"A Bob Nuttall. He lives on the top floor. We knocked on his door, heard someone inside the flat, then realised he'd made his escape using the stairs at the back of the house. He's still on the run."

"Oh, right."

"Are you telling me that he wasn't the person you were referring to?"

"No. I know Paul has had problems with the man on the ground floor before. I can't remember his name. Hang on... it'll come to me."

"What about Nigel Hawkins? Does that ring a bell?"

Sharon nodded vigorously. "Yes, that's the name."

"Problems? Can you tell me what type of problems?"

Sharon's hand covered her mouth as she yawned, then it dropped into her lap. "Nothing that I can pinpoint right now. Paul just mentioned that he was always having bother with him, and that him not paying his rent was the last straw."

"I see." Kayli glanced sideways to make sure Dave was noting down the information, and he was. "What about the other tenants? This Bob Nuttall, for instance. Did your stepfather have any ongoing problems with him?"

Sharon's chubby face contorted a little as she thought. "Maybe. I'm not too sure. To be honest, when Paul spoke about the trouble he was having with his tenants, I tended to switch off from the conversation. Always difficult to know what to say in such circumstances, don't you think?"

"I suppose it must be. Please, try and cast your mind back. It's important that we figure out if anyone has hurt your stepfather on purpose."

"I appreciate that, Inspector. Seriously, I want him found as much as you do. This situation is worrying all of us sick."

"Anita appears to be taking it really badly."

"I'm aware of that. I'm doing my best to ring her when I can, but the last few days, I've been covering a sick friend's night shift, and that means I sleep during the day. When at all possible, that is."

Kayli felt that Sharon was having a dig at her. "I apologise again for inconveniencing you. Can you recall your stepfather falling out with anyone else at the flats? Perhaps a past tenant that he threw out?"

Sharon's eyes widened, and she clicked her fingers together. "There was a chap who wrecked the flat before he moved on. He left owing a couple of months' rent, I believe."

"Can you remember his name, or perhaps you have his forwarding address?" Kayli asked more out of hope than expectation.

"No idea. Like I said, the flats don't concern me."

"It was worth a shot. Can you tell us what flat this particular tenant used to occupy?"

She shook her head. "I can't. No. Sorry."

"Never mind. We'll go back and question the tenants, see if any of them can recall the man's name or know where he moved on to."

"Is there anything else I can help you with?"

"Not at this time. Not unless you can think of anyone else who has caused problems in your stepfather's life recently."

"I can't. Other than what I've told you already."

Kayli stood up, ready to leave. "Then we'll leave you to get some sleep. We really appreciate you taking the time to speak with us today. We'll drop over and see your brother now. He works at the Old Swan in the city centre, right?"

"He does."

They reached the front door. "Here's my card, should you think of anything else that we might find useful."

"Thanks." She tucked the card in the pocket of her robe and held open the door for them to leave.

"One last thing. Try and make contact with Anita today if you can."

Sharon nodded. "I'll see if I can ring her later."

"Thank you for that. Goodbye."

Dave followed Kayli out of the house, and they returned to the car. Once he was seated, Dave said, "That was odd."

Kayli looked at him and frowned. "What was?"

"The way she referred to her stepfather by his first name."

Kayli chuckled. "I wouldn't say it was that unusual. Maybe I'm wrong about that, though."

"Didn't you say that he'd virtually brought them up from a young age? It's not as if he took the family on when they were in their teens. I could understand it if that was the case."

"Hmm… maybe. I'm not that convinced, Dave."

"Okay. It just struck me as odd. Are we going to see the brother now?"

"Yep, it's not far."

~ ~ ~

Kayli parked in the pub's car park and waited for Dave to exit the vehicle before she walked towards the entrance. It was only nine forty-five, and she gambled on the front entrance being locked. She knocked hard on the door at the back. It was a while before a young man with a fashionably small beard opened the door.

"Can I help? We don't open until eleven."

Kayli flashed her warrant card at the man as Dave arrived behind her. "I'm DI Kayli Bright, and this invalid is my partner, DS Dave Chaplin. We'd like a word with Dylan Potts. Would that be you, sir?"

"It would. Do we have to do this now? I'm dealing with a delivery. If the boss comes back and sees that I haven't completed it, he'll be livid, probably dock my wages."

"We shouldn't take up much of your time. Can we come in?"

Dylan Potts sighed and pushed open the door for them to enter. They followed him into a large bar full of characterful low beams and a large inglenook fireplace at one end. However, it was the carpet that drew Kayli's attention. Its godawful pattern made her eyes swim, but she tried to ignore it and focus on the man in front of her.

"Will this do?"

"Here is fine."

"Mind if I continue to mark off the stock while we chat?"

"If you can concentrate on both at the same time, then no, I have no objection."

He picked up a large sheet of paper and a pen from the bar and approached several boxes in the centre of the room. "What can I help you with?"

"This visit is in connection with Paul Potts's disappearance. We've just come from your home, where we spoke to your sister, Sharon."

"I see." He looked up when Kayli mentioned his sister. "And what did she have to say for herself? She should have been in bed."

"Sharon was in bed when we arrived. She kindly spoke to us for about twenty minutes. Perhaps you can fill in some blanks for us."

"Blanks? I don't understand."

"Okay, I really don't want to go over everything your sister told us. However, she did mention that Paul evicted someone from the flats recently. Perhaps you can tell us the person's name so that we can have a chat with them."

He ran two fingers around his mouth, following the shape of his beard. "Funny, I don't recall the incident."

"That's a shame. Maybe you can tell us if your stepfather has had any problems with the tenants in the past. I should have asked rather than told you that snippet of information in the first place."

"When wasn't he having problems with the tenants, you mean? They're all a bunch of no-marks. A waste of space, the lot of them. I warned him not to take on people who were on the Social, but would he listen? No, and now this has happened."

"Are you saying that you believe one of the tenants has done something to your stepfather?"

"Isn't that what you think? That's why you're here, right?"

"We're leaning towards thinking that. However, we need to find the evidence to back up such claims before we can act upon them."

Dylan pointed at a few of the bottles in the box at his feet. "Two… three… four Jim Beam." He looked up at Kayli and tapped his chin with the pen. "What do you need to know that my sister hasn't already told you, Inspector?"

"Your sister mentioned that one of the tenants left the property in a state and owing your father rent."

"My *step*father," he corrected her.

"Sorry, my mistake. Can you tell me what the tenant's name was and which flat he used to occupy?"

"No. I can't, because I have a life of my own. My stepfather refuses to listen to any advice I have to offer about the flats and the way they are run. Therefore, I keep my nose out."

"Does your father—sorry, stepfather—discuss the flats and the running of them with anyone else, in that case? Perhaps his brother, Samuel?"

"More than likely. Again, that was never any of my concern."

"Okay, I can see you're distracted. One final question if I may?"

Dylan inhaled a large breath. "If you must, not that I know anything regarding the flats."

"Actually, two questions. The first is, has your stepfather ever mention the name Bob Nuttall to you?"

"Nope," he replied swiftly. "Next?"

"Apart from the flats and the tenants he deals with, has your stepfather fallen out with anyone else that you know of in recent months?"

"Not that I know of. As I've tried to tell you already, we aren't that close, not really."

"Is that since your mother died?"

"I don't recall us ever being close, if I'm honest. It was different for my sisters. I cared for him because he took us on when he married my mother, but I can't honestly say that I ever loved him. That doesn't mean to say that I'm not upset now that he's gone missing—I am. If I could get the time off work, I would be out there searching for him, if only for my sisters' sakes."

"I understand." Kayli fished out a card and placed it on the bar beside him. "Ring me if you think of anything else. Sorry to get in your way. We'll leave you in peace before your boss returns."

He showed them out the back door again and closed it quickly behind them without saying goodbye.

"Crikey! I'm glad I don't work for an ogre of a boss. He couldn't get rid of us quick enough, could he?" Dave muttered.

"I'll remind you that you uttered those words the next time you think I'm treating you harshly."

"Me and my big mouth. What now?"

"I think we should drop back to the flats and see if we can find out who this mystery tenant is. I also want to check Bob Nuttall's flat again, see if he's resurfaced."

"Want me to stay outside in case Nuttall tries to do a runner again?" Dave asked as he and Kayli slipped back into the car.

"Good idea, although not sure you're going to be much use preventing him doing a runner again."

"I can trip him up." Dave tapped one of his crutches. "These guys are nifty for doing that."

CHAPTER FIVE

Kayli took a deep breath before she rang the buzzer to Nigel Hawkins's flat. She tapped her foot as she waited for him to answer it. When no answer came, she tried the next name on the list—Stuart Rawlinson.

He answered virtually straight away with an abrupt "Yeah, who is it?"

Kayli couldn't tell if his voice was slurred or if the intercom was playing up. "Hello, Mr. Rawlinson. This is DI Kayli Bright. Would you mind letting me in?"

"What the heck? Why? You asked all your questions yesterday."

"Something else has come up in our enquiries. If you can just buzz me in. Thanks."

He muttered something indecipherable before the buzzer sounded to unlock the door. Kayli pulled it open and stopped outside Nigel Hawkins's flat first. She banged her fist on the door. When she got no answer, she made her way up the stairs to Stuart Rawlinson's flat and knocked on the door. He looked dreadful when he opened the door, stoned out of his mind, and the smell of drugs coming from his flat quickly overwhelmed her.

"Are you doing drugs, Mr. Rawlinson?"

"Me? Not me, love. Never touch the damn things. I've got some incense sticks burning. That's what you can smell." He waved his hand around. "Bit overpowering for you? Sorry, lass."

Kayli narrowed her eyes and shook her head at him. "Because if it's drugs I'm smelling, I'd have to take you in, sir."

He nodded. "Yes, oh yes, of course you would and rightly so," he slurred and slouched against the doorframe. "You said something about making further enquiries?"

"I did. I was hoping to come in for a chat, but I think I'll forget that now. Going back to my visit yesterday, can you tell me about a tenant who used to live here who Mr. Potts asked to leave recently?"

"What was the name?"

"That's the problem—I don't have a clue. Can you recall someone leaving the building?"

He ran a hand through his messed-up hair. "I think so. Can't for the life of me give you a name, though. Sorry."

"Not to worry. I'll try some of the other flats. By the way, have you seen Bob Nuttall on the top floor since yesterday?"

"Nope. I tend to keep to meself. Sorry, love." He was already closing the door before she had the chance to say thank you.

Kayli stuck her foot out to prevent the door from closing. "If you'll take some advice, Mr. Rawlinson, I'd get your priorities in order, knock the drugs on the head and put the money to good use, like paying the rent you owe."

"I told you already, it's incense you can smell, not drugs. Never touch the stuff."

Kayli shook her head and removed her foot to allow him to shut the door. She moved on to the neighbour's flat and knocked on the door. She smiled when Colleen Porter answered. "Hello again. Sorry to disturb you. I just wondered if I could have a quick chat."

"Of course. Would you like to come in?"

"Wonderful, thank you. No baby today?"

"I've just put him down for a little nap. Neither of us slept well last night, and he's a bit grouchy." Colleen closed the door quietly behind Kayli and walked into the first room they came to. "It's not much, but it's home for now."

"You've got it looking nice. Have you lived here long?"

"Coming up to two months." She lowered her voice and leaned forward. "Think I'm going to be moving on soon. Not sure I like being the only woman in this block. It can be quite unsettling at times."

"I can imagine. Have you ever had any bother from any of the other tenants?"

"Not directly. I just think men can be really selfish at times. They all know I've got a child, but they're totally inconsiderate. You know, banging doors and either playing music or listening to the TV loudly at all hours. I know a lot of them don't work, but why do they have to be so damn pig-headed about things?"

"That's such a shame. I'd offer to have a word with them for you, except I doubt they would listen to me, and they'd probably make things a whole lot worse if they knew you'd complained about them. A catch-22 situation."

"It really isn't worth the hassle. Can I ask why you've come back so soon?"

"We hit on something to do with our case and needed to clarify it. I'm guessing that you took over from someone who'd recently vacated the flat."

"That's right. When Mr. Potts showed me the flat, he told me that he'd had to virtually tear it back to its bare bones because the last tenant had wrecked the place. I was thrilled, as you can imagine. This place is lovely. I doubt I'll find another flat in this condition in the future."

"I can imagine. People often disrespect things that belong to others nowadays. Do you think Mr. Potts was trying to change the quality of tenants by allowing you to move in?"

"He said just that when he showed me around the flat. I thought I'd give it a little time for him to implement the changes, but no one else has ever moved in. Not sure I can handle it much longer. I need to let Mr. Potts know that I've made a decision to move on. It might kick him up the backside and force him into giving some of these blokes the boot."

Kayli nodded. "Let's hope Mr. Potts surfaces soon to do just that."

"What are you saying? That he's gone missing?"

"Yes, that's why we were asking questions. To be honest with you, we're not sure if he's gone missing or if anything bad has happened to him. His daughters and son seem to think the latter."

Her hand covered her mouth then dropped into her lap. "That's terrible. And you think someone around here is to blame?"

Kayli shrugged. "Hard to say. All we have is a few witnesses who said they heard raised voices on Saturday evening. Mr. Potts was here around that time and hasn't been heard from or seen since."

The young woman's face drained of all colour. "Oh no. How awful for the family. That's it. I'm definitely going to move out now if you're telling me it's not safe around here."

"Sorry, I didn't mean to frighten you. The trouble is we have no evidence to prove anything untoward has happened to Mr. Potts. The person who left the flat before you moved in—can you tell me his or her name?"

"Hang on, I think I had a letter come for them a week or so ago. I've been too busy to do anything about it. I was supposed to give it to Mr. Potts the next time I saw him." She left her chair and walked out of the room. She returned carrying an envelope a few moments later. "Here you go, a Harry Sims."

"I don't suppose you know if he left a forwarding address?"

She sat down on the sofa again. "Sorry, no. I've had a couple of letters, the brown-envelope kind, for him, and I've always given them to Mr. Potts to deal with."

Kayli sighed. "That's a shame... never mind. At least we've got a name to go on now."

"I hope it helps. Mr. Potts was really upset by the damage the man caused before he moved out."

"I'm not surprised. It must be heartbreaking to let out your property only for someone to trash it. Oh well, I better get on and see if I can get any more details about Mr. Sims from the other tenants. Thanks for your help."

Colleen walked her to the front door. "If you hear of any nice flats in a decent area going cheap, let me know."

Kayli smiled. "I'll keep my ear to the ground for you. Hope you find somewhere more suitable soon."

"Thanks, me too. Good luck with your investigation. I hope you find Mr. Potts soon. He seems a nice old man. Can't believe that someone would deliberately set out to harm him."

"Thanks. We'll see where the investigation leads us. Take care of yourself and the little one."

Kayli decided to creep up the stairs and stand outside Bob Nuttall's flat, her ear pressed up against the door, hoping to hear some movement inside. She was unlucky. All was silent. Kayli knocked on the door then listened again. Still nothing. Defeated, she descended the two flights of stairs and left the building. She went round the side and up the alley, where she found Dave leaning against a wall at the rear of the property. "Anything?"

Dave shook his head. "Nope. All quiet."

"Okay. Let's not hang around here, then. I've got a name for us to look into back at the station."

"Sounds promising. The previous tenant?"

"Yep. Come on, matey. Hop to it."

~ ~ ~

They drove back to the station. As soon as Kayli stepped through the door of the incident room, Graeme looked up and motioned for her to join him. Her heart rate sped up. "I'm hoping this means that you've located Potts's car."

"You'd be right, boss. Here it is, getting on the M5. I've tracked its route, and it left the motorway here, in Almondsbury. The car travelled along the M48 over the river and into Wales. That's as far as I've got for now. Just wanted to bring you up to date."

"Excellent news. What about the driver? Can you see who is driving the car, Graeme?"

"It's obscured. The ANPR cameras are only picking up the torso of the person driving the vehicle. There are no headshots."

"Are you telling me it could be a male or female driving the car?"

"I am."

"Maybe we should contact the police around that area."

Graeme shrugged. "And tell them what? Let me try and see where the car stops first. I think it would save a lot of time. Wales is a pretty big area, boss."

"I know. I suppose my eagerness is getting the better of me."

Dave walked into the room.

"This will cheer you up. Graeme has spotted Potts's car. The bad news is it was heading into Wales."

Dave smirked then shook his head. "Okay, I managed to bite my tongue before I spouted anything derogatory."

"Glad to hear it," Kayli said, glaring at him. "What about you, Donna? Oh wait, I have another name for you to do a background check on for me. A Harry Sims. He was the tenant who Potts asked to leave. He showed his dislike for that idea by wrecking the flat. I have no forwarding address. See what you can find out about him, if you would."

"I'll do my best. I'm still going through the background checks. Nothing suspicious has shown up regarding the family yet. Samuel Potts was in the navy, based in Plymouth for around twenty-five years. Perfect record. Nothing to report there."

"I didn't think there would be. He came across to me as a really likeable character. Not every brother I know keeps in touch with his sibling daily."

"I agree. Let me do a brief search on Sims, and I'll get back to you ASAP."

Kayli walked into her office. To occupy her mind, she threw herself into paperwork. Otherwise, she would have been sorely tempted to keep pestering the team every five minutes. Around twenty minutes later, Donna appeared in the doorway of Kayli's office.

"I hope you have some good news. I could definitely do with it after tackling this crap."

Donna smiled. "Yes and no. I have a Harry Sims showing up as being deceased."

"Bloody hell. When are we going to catch a frigging break on this one? We have no way of knowing if it's the Sims we're after, right?"

"I can see if I can dig back some more, try to find if there's a social security number logging him at the flats. Leave it with me."

"Thanks, Donna. Before you go, what date was his death? Can we get any indication from that?"

"According to the death certificate, around six weeks ago."

"Any address logged?"

"Nope, looks like he was homeless and got in a scrap. He died in hospital with numerous knife wounds. The one that proved fatal was the one to his lungs."

"Okay, thanks for the info, Donna. I really wouldn't bother wasting your time searching any further. Not if he died six weeks ago."

"I'll get back to looking into the family's background then."

"Let me know what you find out."

Donna nodded and left the office.

Kayli returned to her paperwork but was disturbed a few moments later when the phone on her desk rang. "DI Bright. Can I help you?"

"It's Control here, ma'am. My system has flagged up to contact you if we locate an Opel Manta with the registration number B520 6OX."

Excited, Kayli sat forward in her chair. "And?"

"We've located the vehicle down by the river at the Saint Philips Trade Centre."

"Just the vehicle, or was anyone inside?"

"Only the vehicle, ma'am."

"Have you got the postcode?"

The operator reeled it off.

"No one is to go near the vehicle. Can you pass on that message?"

"I will, ma'am. I take it you'll be attending the scene?"

"On my way now." Kayli hung up and rushed out of the office. "Dave, they've located Nuttall's car. Do you want to come with me?"

Dave was on his feet in a flash. "Too bloody right. Where?"

"I'll fill you in on the details on the way."

Kayli flew down the stairs, started the car, inserted the postcode in the satnav and pulled up outside the entrance of the station before Dave arrived. He appeared within seconds and jumped in. Kayli put her foot down as soon as he closed the door.

"Where did they find it?" he asked. "Was Nuttall there?"

Kayli shook her head and came to a halt at a red light. "Down at the Saint Philips Trade Centre near the river, and no, Nuttall wasn't there."

"Great. So why are we rushing down there then?"

"The last thing I want is dozens of people crawling over the vehicle. I also want to survey the area for myself."

"Fair enough."

Kayli navigated the traffic and pulled up alongside the Opel around fifteen minutes later. The driver's door was open, and the keys were hanging in the ignition when Kayli and Dave approached the vehicle.

Using their patrol car, two officers had cordoned off the area. Kayli surveyed the road and went down the bank towards the river.

Dave remained on the road and called down, "Are you thinking he jumped?"

Kayli shrugged, lost deep in thought. It was a strange location for someone to drive up to only to leave their vehicle. *Did Nuttall jump as Dave had suggested? Or was he due to meet someone? A possible exchange, perhaps involving Potts.* The scenarios were endless and all very perplexing for Kayli to make any sense out of. All she was sure about was that certain elements to this case just didn't add up.

"What are you thinking?" Dave shouted.

"How can a missing persons case have so many puzzling issues surrounding it? It's bloody driving me nuts. Did Nuttall have anything to do with Paul Potts going missing? Was the argument just a coincidence? Nuttall taking off like that, why would he do it?"

"It's all a damn mystery. Do you think he's in the river? Want me to call in the dive team?"

Kayli held her arms out to the side and slapped them against her thighs. "Would it be worth it? What if he's not in there? It would be a total waste of funds, right?"

"I guess." Dave looked in the direction of the nearby buildings. "I can't even see any CCTV cameras facing this way."

"Bugger. That's not helpful. Stay there. I'm going to take a walk. See if I can see anything farther down the river. I'll be back soon."

"Be careful. Want me to send one of the constables to accompany you?"

"I'll be fine. You worry too much," she called back over her shoulder.

"Yeah, it's only because I care."

Kayli chuckled at his response. She walked along the edge of the river for almost half a mile before she turned back. She could make out nothing that seemed to be evidence, and there were no bodies tucked along the water's edge in the reeds.

She climbed up the bank and trotted along the road until she reached the vehicle. Pulling on a pair of blue latex gloves, she approached the Opel and turned the key in the ignition. The car was dead, no hint of a spark to start it up. Kayli glanced down at the fuel gauge. It was in the red. She slapped the top of the car and heaved a frustrated sigh. "There's our answer. He ran out of petrol.

Probably took off without his wallet and has been driving around until he had no petrol left. I think it's time we got a warrant to search his address."

"On what grounds?"

"Avoiding talking to the police. We've also got witnesses telling us that he had an argument with Potts before he was reported missing. That should cover it."

"I'll get Donna on it right away. She can get Forensics to pick the car up too."

"Good idea. We need to get back. I want us all looking at the CCTV on this one. Our priority has to be to find out in which direction Nuttall went and if he left his vehicle alone or if he was accompanied by anyone."

"By anyone, I take it you're referring to Paul Potts?"

"Of course. Come on, Dave, shake a leg." Kayli grinned when he rolled his eyes at the dour joke.

~ ~ ~

Kayli called for Donna's and Graeme's attention as soon as she and Dave arrived back in the incident room. "Graeme, I need you to put on hold tracing Potts's car for the moment and concentrate on locating Nuttall. Find out what CCTV cameras are working around the trading estate. I'm thinking he set off on foot, although I might be wrong about that, as he could've possibly rung someone to pick him up from the location. We need to confirm that ASAP." Kayli swivelled to address Donna. "Any news on the warrant yet, Donna?"

"I requested it as soon as Dave rang in. They said it should be ready sometime this afternoon. Couldn't give me a definite time, though."

"Okay. Until then, I'd like us all to help Graeme search through the CCTV. Can you hook a few computers up at the same time for us, Graeme?"

"I can do that. Give me ten minutes, maybe a little longer." Graeme left his chair and turned on a few of the nearby monitors to warm up.

Kayli wandered over to the whiteboard and updated it while she waited, to avoid impatiently pacing the room.

Graeme worked swiftly and announced he was finished soon enough. Together, the four of them tackled the task in hand. It wasn't long before Graeme, the expert in this field, came up trumps. "I've got him. At least I think it's him."

"Donna, can you print off a copy of his photo from his record for me?"

The printer churned out Nuttall's image a few seconds later. Donna collected it and held it up close to the monitor for everyone to compare the images.

Kayli nodded. "That's our guy. He's heading from the trading estate, right, Graeme?"

"That's right. I'm just going to speed it up a little to see where he's heading. There are no other vehicles around at present."

Kayli watched through narrowed eyes and studied the man's demeanour. He looked shifty from the outset, constantly looking over his shoulder as if he knew the police would be after him. "Damn, damn, damn, he's heading into a busy pedestrianised area."

"Hang on. Yes, he's going to hop on the bus," Dave pointed out.

"That's all we need. Can you get the bus number, Graeme?"

"Leave it with me, boss. I'll figure it out and get in touch with the bus company. All the buses nowadays are fitted with cameras anyway, so all is not lost just yet."

Kayli nodded and walked across the room to buy coffees for the team.

The phone rang on Donna's desk as Kayli placed a cup beside her.

"Hello. DC Donna Travis... That's wonderful news. Thank you for rushing it through for me." Donna ended the call. "The warrant is through. I asked them to hurry things along for me, told them it was urgent."

"Good job, Donna. Right, Dave, drink up, and we'll get back to the flats."

"Bloody hell, we might as well get a room at that place, the amount of time we're spending there."

"Stop moaning."

CHAPTER SIX

Kayli held the passenger door open for Dave once they arrived at the flats. Dave was right: their visits to this place were becoming a habit. Hopefully, it would be the last time they had to call back there, in connection with the case anyway.

Once they were both up the steps, Kayli buzzed Colleen's flat to gain access to the building.

A cautious voice came through the speaker.

"Colleen, it's DI Bright again. Sorry to disturb you, but can you buzz me in, please?"

The door clunked, and Dave pushed it open with his crutch. Kayli led the way up one flight of stairs. Colleen was standing by her door with her child on her hip.

"Everything all right?" she asked anxiously.

"Nothing to be concerned about. We've obtained a warrant to search Bob Nuttall's flat. I don't suppose you've heard him come back during the day, have you?"

"No, sorry. It's been really quiet up there. Good luck. I hope you find what you're looking for."

"So do I." Kayli smiled and continued up the next flight of stairs to the top floor. She waited for Dave to arrive and asked, "How are we going to break down the door?"

"Shame to do that. I don't suppose the family will be too happy about that."

She tapped on the door, just in case Nuttall was home, not that he would have opened the door to them. "Not sure it will matter to them as long as we find out what has happened to Paul. Are you up for this? Or do you want me to do my GI Jane bit again?" Kayli chuckled.

Dave tutted, placed one of his crutches up against the wall and shoulder-charged the door. It refused to budge. He put more power behind the charge and almost toppled over when the door gave in. Kayli caught hold of his arm to prevent him from falling over. She handed him his other crutch, and together, they entered the room.

The room was a tip. It was a bedsit more than a flat. The cluttered kitchen area was piled high with dirty dishes and cutlery. The single bed in the far corner had been left unmade, and the sheets looked filthy, as if they hadn't seen the inside of a washing machine in months. The TV was on standby, as was the small DVD player beside it. Alongside that were numerous DVD cases.

"I really don't want to know what's on them," Kayli said, her nose wrinkling in distaste.

Dave bent down to pick up the top DVD and grinned at her. "Yep, you were right. Pirated copies of porn. Some bird with bazookas the size of large Atlas stones. They look just as heavy too."

"All right, Dave, spare me the details. My imagination has already dealt with that. It doesn't look like he's returned at all. Although that's pretty hard to determine."

"Except that the fire escape door is still ajar."

"Well spotted. Put on your gloves. We'll tear this place apart. I wouldn't worry about making a mess, either. If anything, it'll probably be an improvement."

Kayli searched the single wardrobe in the opposite corner to the bed. The smell of sour body odour almost knocked her off her feet. "Jesus, does this place even have a bathroom? By the smell of this, I'd say Nuttall hasn't washed in months, either himself or his clothes."

Dave pulled a face. "There's a door over there. I'm presuming that'll be the loo and the shower. God, this place is the pits." He walked towards the door and stuck his head round it. "Jesus! That's gross. The loo is full with—"

"Stop! I don't want to know. Anything else in there?"

"A shower that looks barely used. That figures, right?" He slammed the door behind him.

"Okay, let's not hang around. I'll check through the drawers. Hope I don't find any dirty underwear staring back at me."

Dave chuckled and moved towards the bed. He opened the drawer to the bedside table and whistled. "Bingo! I think we hit the jackpot."

Kayli rushed across the small room to join him. "Holy crap! There must be thousands there."

"Too bloody right."

Dave withdrew the large bundle of twenty-pound notes from the drawer and popped the cash into a see-through plastic evidence bag. He took a photo on his phone, something Kayli always insisted on doing with large sums of cash, just in case the money went missing once it was placed in the evidence storeroom. That had happened over the years when the force was riddled with bent coppers. Thankfully, Kayli hadn't come across any incidents of that kind in the past few years.

"All right... well, this begs the question of why would Nuttall run without at least grabbing a handful of cash first. If he had any money with him, he wouldn't have dumped his car when it ran out of petrol, right?"

"The plot thickens. What if he was keeping the money stashed away for someone?"

"Would you trust the likes of him?" Kayli asked, shaking her head.

"Hey, there must be a certain code of honour amongst criminals."

Kayli shrugged. "If you say so. All right, what about this scenario, then... if Nuttall had all this cash on him, then why did he and Potts have an argument on Saturday about non-payment of his rent?"

Dave raised an eyebrow. "Maybe the money came into his hands *after* Saturday."

"What? As some form of payment in connection with Potts going missing?"

He hitched up a shoulder. "Who knows? It's just a theory."

"A very good theory, and one that we need to investigate further," Kayli replied, holding up the bag to inspect the contents. "I'd say there's at least twenty thousand here."

"If it is as we suspect, maybe someone employed him as a hitman."

Kayli placed the bag back on the bed and rubbed the side of her face. "A hitman would indicate that we're talking about someone who knows Paul Potts well."

Dave pointed at her. "A family member?"

Kayli sighed heavily. "In other cases, perhaps. I'm not so certain about that in this instance. Bugger, let's hope we find Nuttall soon so that he can clarify things for us."

"Want to carry on searching? We might find a letter of sorts or possible instructions from someone."

Kayli scanned the room. "Where else can we check? Except..." She stamped on the floor with her foot and looked around the room at the edges of the carpet to see if any showed signs of being disturbed.

"You thinking under the floorboards?"

"Yep, except I can't see any indication of where that might be. Maybe I'm barking up the wrong tree. Only one way to find out." Kayli went to the corner of the room and found a frayed area of carpet, which she pulled on. The carpet frayed a little more but released from the gripper rod soon enough. She folded it back to the middle of the room before it hit the bed then searched for any possible loose floorboards. "Can't see anything, can you?"

"What about that one, close to the wall? It seems a little raised compared to the others."

"I see it." Kayli took a few steps then crouched down again to test the board, which rocked under her hand. She took a penknife that Mark insisted she carry from her pocket and levered the floorboard out of position. "Bloody Nora! There's more money stuffed down here."

"How much? Any idea?"

Kayli shook her head and removed another evidence bag from her pocket. She reached into the hole and extracted another three bundles of twenties. "Crap, looks like the same amount in each one as you found in the drawer."

"Eighty grand? What the fuck would this guy be doing with that sort of money?"

"The question is, partner, is the money from the same pay-out or separate negotiations?"

"Crap, this is getting worse by the minute. I think we should call in a forensics team, let them tear this place apart. I dread to think what we might find behind the walls."

"Oh God, don't say that. You're right. I'm going to give them a call now."

Kayli punched a number into her phone, which directed her to the lab immediately. She gave their location, reported what they had found and asked for a team of analysts to come to the flat as soon as possible. She was told to expect them within half an hour. "As tempting as it might be for us to continue this search, I think it would be better to wait for the experts to arrive. Did you get a photo of the rest of the dosh we found?"

"Yep, while you were on the phone."

"I need some fresh air." Kayli stepped out onto the fire escape. If only things were different. If only Dave had been guarding the back alley. *If ifs and ands and pots and pans, as Mum always says.* She went back inside the flat and paced the floor until the forensics team arrived.

It was almost four o'clock before the forensics team showed up. Kayli rushed down the stairs to open the door for the two men, already suited and booted in their protective clothing. "Thanks for coming, gents. The flat is the penthouse suite on the top floor."

The two men looked at each other and back at her. "This place has a penthouse?" the older man asked incredulously.

"I'm jesting. You'll need your sense of humour to see through this task, gents, believe me."

The three of them walked up the two flights of stairs and into the room. "Jesus, you weren't kidding," the older man said. "Can I ask how much of this mess you made?"

Kayli chuckled. "Aside from pulling up the carpet, not much. We found it in this state, I can assure you. Dave, show the gents what we've found, please."

Her partner held up the two bags containing the money.

Both the forensics guys whistled. "Holy crap! There must be— what? A hundred grand there?"

"We haven't counted it, but we don't think that figure's far off. Do you want to photograph it before we take it back to the station?"

The younger of the two technicians bent down to his large case and withdrew a camera, to which he attached a lens, and fired off dozens of shots. "Done. You're free to take it now. Before you go, is there anything in particular you're looking for?"

"I'll give you the low-down on the case. It started out as a missing persons case. The landlord of the flats came here last Saturday to chase three tenants for rent owed. His brother was expecting him to show up at the pub that night sometime after his visit, but he never showed up and hasn't been seen or heard from since. When we came to question the tenants, the guy living in this flat refused to open the door to us and instead absconded down the fire escape, never to be seen again. Actually, that's not quite true. We put out an alert on his car and discovered it a few hours ago, where he'd deserted it after running out of petrol."

One of the technicians laughed. "Don't tell me he ran out of money."

"That's exactly what we think. Maybe he didn't have time to grab some notes before he ran from us. Anyway, I've arranged for you guys to pick up his Opel Manta. It's down at the Saint Philips Trade Centre. I need you guys to go over it thoroughly, if you will."

"Agreed. Leave it with us. We'll contact the lab, make sure it has been picked up."

"Appreciate it. Right, we'll be off and leave this in your capable hands." She handed the older man a business card. "Let me know if you find anything else. Thanks."

"Will do."

Kayli and Dave made their way back down the stairs and out to the car.

"What now?" Dave asked once they were settled in the car.

"Back to the station, I suppose. Hopefully, Graeme will be able to furnish us with more news on Potts's car soon."

"Let's hope so. Without that, I can't see us solving this case. Not unless we pick up Nuttall in the meantime. Is it worth asking the media for help?"

"Maybe. Let's see what news the guys back at base have for us first. I might go down that route tomorrow. Although I suspect using the media could make Nuttall go underground."

They drove back to the station, but Kayli felt the disappointment rising when Graeme told her that he was still trying to track down Potts's car via the ANPR cameras.

She retired to her office to wallow until six o'clock. The team were just packing up, getting ready to leave, when she emerged from the office. "Thanks for all your hard work on this one, guys. Let's hope things really start to kick off tomorrow. See you in the morning."

She watched Graeme and Donna leave, but Dave remained in his seat. She perched her backside on the desk closest to his. "Something wrong, partner? You're usually the first to leave."

He frowned. "I am?"

"All right, I stand corrected. The second person to leave. How's that?"

Dave shrugged. "What are we doing on this case?"

"This is unlike you, Dave. Any specific reason why you should be asking that question after a few days?"

"Not one in particular. You know how it is... certain cases don't sit well with you, and you have no inclination why. Well, I guess this is one of those cases. What if Potts has just taken off? Fed up with his family and felt the need to get away from them?"

"Except he's not that kind of person, according to his brother and his daughter, is he?"

"Yeah, I get that. But if he's stressed out running the flats, maybe he simply decided to throw in the towel, thought it wasn't worth all the aggravation or stress. I know I would feel that way after visiting that dive and the tenants he has living there, or should I say wrecking the place. Nuttall's flat was a shit-tip. It would break my heart if I bought a property and people treated it like that."

"I hear what you're saying, Dave, and don't think the thought hasn't entered my mind. The thing is both his brother and Anita are adamant that this is totally out of character for Paul. I'm sure they would say if he was finding the situation stressful and unable to cope with it."

Dave pulled his crutches towards him and levered himself out of the chair. "I guess you're right." He tapped his temple. "I've just got a niggling little voice up here, chipping away at me."

"Hey, we wouldn't be coppers if we didn't have a certain amount of that going on in our heads during a case, right?"

They walked towards the exit. "I suppose. What are your plans tonight? Feet up with the new hubby, with a glass of wine?"

Kayli shook her head as she switched off the lights and closed the door behind her. "Hardly. I doubt I'll see much of Mark over the next few days. He starts his new job tonight."

"Damn, sorry. I forgot about that. Is he still on the lookout for another job? I can't see him sticking with that career for long, given his experience."

"He says he is still looking. Who knows? He might end up enjoying throwing troublemakers out of a nightclub."

Dave shook his head and laughed. "I doubt it. I'll give him until the end of next week."

"Let's just say I'd rather have him employed than sat at home, feeling sorry for himself. It was a nightmare living with him before he took that security job in Afghanistan."

"You guys are made for each other. I'm sure Mark will find a more suitable job soon and everything will be hunky-dory again."

"I wish I had your faith. Come on. Let's go home. Say hi to Suranne and Luke for me."

CHAPTER SEVEN

Feeling weary, Kayli slipped her key in the front door and pushed it open. "Hi, honey. I'm home."

Mark appeared swiftly at the entrance to the lounge and leaned against the doorframe. His smile, showing off his gleaming white teeth, proved to her how much he'd missed her.

She sashayed towards him, flung her arms around his neck and kissed him. "Hello, you. Have you missed me?"

"I have. Good day?" He pulled away from her and headed into the lounge.

Her nose rose into the air to smell the aroma of their evening meal. "So-so. You've cooked again. I could get used to this. What have we got?"

"Cottage pie. At least, it's supposed to be, but the mashed potato sank into the mixture. It don't look pretty."

Kayli laughed. "Oops. If it tastes as good as it smells, we're in for a treat."

"Do you want to dish the mess up?"

"If you want me to." Kayli walked into the kitchen and placed her hands in the oven gloves. "Can you get the plates out for me?"

"They're in the bottom of the oven, keeping warm."

"I've trained you well." She opened the oven and chuckled when she saw the mess confronting her. Mark wasn't wrong—the meal looked terrible. The smell was fantastic, though, and it pushed aside her doubts as she withdrew the Pyrex dish from the oven and placed it on the chopping board on the worktop. Then she switched off the oven and removed the plates. Once she'd dished up the cottage pie and the accompanying vegetables, consisting of cabbage and carrots, Kayli called for him to join her.

Mark entered the room, looking a little sheepish. "It's a disaster, right?"

"Nope, I'm sure it'll be fine. Here you go." She placed the sloppy mess in front of him.

He studied it from every angle before he plucked up the courage to take his first mouthful. "Wow, actually, it tastes amazing, even if I do say so myself. Any idea what I did wrong?"

"I'm not one to criticise such a sterling effort, but I think perhaps you needed to either thicken the gravy or wait for the bottom mixture to have cooled down before you added the mashed potato on the top. Not that I'm an expert chef, of course."

"I think you're right. I didn't even think about thickening the gravy. Maybe I put too much milk in the potato too. I'll know next time."

"Glad the experience hasn't put you off making future meals. It's all trial and error when we begin preparing meals. I'm just grateful that you're willing to give it a go. A lot of men would be sitting on their arses, waiting for their wives to come home and fix the meal for them."

His gaze met hers. "You mean like I used to do before going out there."

Kayli smiled at him. "I didn't like to say that. Yes, like you used to do. I'm glad Afghanistan changed you in some ways."

"I am too. I appreciate you more, for one thing. I've been a bastard to you this past year or so, something that I plan on making up for in the future."

She reached across the table for his hand. He inserted his fingers through hers, and they held on firmly.

"You don't have to do that. We came through the dreadful experience, and that's all that matters. We need to ensure we enjoy life to its fullest now. Life is far too short."

They ate the rest of their meal one-handed, with their other hands linked. After eating, Kayli cleared up the kitchen while Mark went upstairs to change for work. He rejoined her as she was putting the last dishes away in the cupboard.

"Well, what do you think?" he asked, twirling on the spot in his evening suit and dicky bow tie.

Her heart skipped several beats. He looked very handsome, too handsome to be standing on the door of a nightclub. "Wow, you look amazing. I have a feeling you're going to attract the attention of the girls too."

He took three steps and placed his hands on the top of her arms. "I only have eyes for one girl in this world. Got that?"

She lifted her mouth to his. "Got that. After what we've been through, who could possibly doubt the love we feel for each other."

"Exactly. I want to grow old and grey with you, Mrs. Wren. Hey, that reminds me. Aren't you going to change your name at work?"

"I thought about it and decided against it for now. Is that okay? It's a lot of bother, loads of paperwork involved, and I have enough of that to deal with on a daily basis. I couldn't handle any more."

He kissed the top of her head. "Whatever suits you. I'm more than happy to go along with that. I better shoot off now. They want me there early on the first night to show me the ropes."

"That's a shame. Think of me curled up in front of the boring TV tonight now and again, won't you?"

"You'll be constantly on my mind. I promise you. There are plenty of films to see if you fancy one."

"Not sure I fancy an action movie tonight. I'll be fine. Don't worry about me. I'll have a nice soak in the bath and an early night, I think, with a good book. Enjoy the peace and quiet."

"I can't promise I'll get a chance to ring you, but if I do, you know I'll do it."

"Not too late, though. What time do you think you'll be home?"

His lip lifted at the side. "Around three to three thirty."

"Ouch! Try not to wake me when you come in, and I'll try not to wake you when I leave in the morning. It's going to be tough getting used to our new routine."

He shrugged. "We're going to have to get used to it for now, until something better comes along."

"I hope that elusive job turns up soon. I love you, Mark Wren."

"I love you too, Kayli Bright-Wren."

"Ooo… I like the sound of that."

"So do I. It might be good to have a double-barrelled surname. We should mull that over."

"I was kidding, but I think the idea has legs. I wonder if it's possible to do that. We'll have to delve into it."

"I'll leave you to do that. I can't hang around here, chatting. I have to get off now. See you later."

One last kiss, then he was gone. Almost immediately, Kayli felt the room closing in on her, suffocating her. She hated being by herself, and she'd spent months alone in the house with Mark miles away. *Hang in there. It won't be for long.*

Kayli trudged up the stairs to run a bath. She had just placed the plug in the hole when her mobile rang. She turned on the tap and left the bathroom before she answered the call. "What did you forget?" she asked, thinking it was Mark ringing her.

"Kayli, it's me."

"Giles? What's wrong?" She could tell by the seriousness of her brother's tone that something was up.

"Annabelle is bleeding. I'm setting off for the hospital and wondered if you could come over and look after Bobby for us."

"Oh shit! Is it the baby? Forget that. Stupid question. I'll be there in ten minutes."

"You're a treasure. Drive carefully."

"Give her a hug from me."

Kayli flung open the bathroom door, turned off the tap and let the water out the bath. Then she ran downstairs, grabbed her handbag and coat and flew out the front door. Her mind was working overtime during the trip to her brother's house. When she arrived, an ambulance was parked outside the house. She ran past it and in through the front door. The paramedics were in the process of placing Annabelle on a stretcher rather than in a wheelchair.

"Annabelle, I'm so sorry. They'll look after you at the hospital."

Annabelle reached for Kayli's hand and squeezed it tightly. With tears brimming in her eyes, she whispered, "Thanks for coming. I think it's too late. Look after Bobby for me."

Kayli bent down and kissed Annabelle's cheek. "Don't worry about Bobby. I'll take care of him." She backed up when the paramedics indicated they were ready to leave. Kayli hugged her shell-shocked brother and pushed him in the back. "Go. She needs you. Bobby is in safe hands, love."

"What am I going to do or say, Kayli?"

"Don't think about that now. Just be with her, Giles. Ring me as soon as you hear anything."

"I will." He nodded, his face void of colour.

Kayli tried her hardest to remain strong, but her heart was breaking for her brother and her wonderful sister-in-law.

"Bobby's in his room. Take care of him. Tell him we love him if he wakes up. I'll be in touch soon. Thank you for coming over."

"Just go," she ordered, pointing at the ambulance. The paramedics were waiting to close the back door.

She stood at the front door and watched the vehicle pull away from the house. Kayli kicked herself—she should have asked her brother if he'd rung their parents to fill them in. She decided to go upstairs to check on Bobby then ring her parents once she was sure Bobby was asleep. She tiptoed into the little man's room and leaned over his bed. One eye opened to look at her.

"Hello, sweetie. Can't you sleep?"

"I want my mummy," Bobby sobbed, rubbing at his eyes.

Kayli lifted back the quilt and cuddled him, but he wriggled out of her grasp. "No, don't want you. I want my mummy."

Kayli smiled at her nephew, who in the last few months had shown signs that he was accepting her. "Mummy and Daddy had to go out, sweetie. But I'm here to look after you."

Bobby broke down in tears. He raised his legs and kicked Kayli out of the bed.

She landed with a thump on her backside. "Oww… Bobby, you hurt Aunty Kayli."

"Good. I don't want you. I want my mummy."

Kayli stood up and removed her mobile from her pocket. She left the room and rang her mother from the hallway. She was in unknown territory. Bobby was still only just getting used to her when he was a happy child, running around and bringing her toys to play with. Knowing how to handle him when the poor mite was obviously in distress was another matter entirely.

"Hello. Is that you, Kayli?"

Kayli rushed down the hallway and into the master bedroom. "Yes, Mum. I'm so sorry to ring you like this, but I got a call from

Giles a little while ago to say that Annabelle needed to go to hospital, and he asked me to come over and sit with Bobby—"

Her mother gasped. "Oh my! Hospital? I hope it's nothing serious, dear. Silly statement, I know, as neither Giles nor Annabelle would bother the hospital if something wasn't wrong."

"The thing is, Mum, Bobby was awake when I got here, and I think he's sensing something is wrong and is refusing to let me comfort him. I was wondering if you had any ideas what I can do to make him trust me, if that is even the right word. I tried getting into bed with him to give him a cuddle, but he was having none of that and soon kicked me out."

"Oh dear, that's not good. Why don't you both jump in the car and come over here. I'll make up the spare bed for him. He'll soon settle down once his grandfather starts reading to him. Make sure you bring a couple of bedtime stories with you. His favourites are usually sitting on the bedside table next to him."

"You're a lifesaver, Mum. You don't think Giles will be angry with me, do you?"

"What on earth for? He'll probably be delighted you thought to seek help with the situation rather than have Bobby in a state. Come on. Get off the phone and into the car."

"Oh no. I've just had a thought. I don't have a car seat for him."

Her mother sighed. "Okay, your father has one in his car. Stay where you are, and he'll come over there and bring you back here. Problem solved."

"You have a solution for everything. Thanks, Mum. Shall I get Bobby dressed or leave him as he is?"

"Leave him in his pyjamas and make sure you wrap him up well in his thick dressing gown and also put his coat on. The last thing we want is for him to come down with a cold."

"If he'll let me near him, I'll make sure I do that. See you soon. Thanks, Mum." Kayli ended the call and tiptoed, retracing her steps to Bobby's bedroom. She pushed the door open a little and cringed when the hinges squeaked.

Little Bobby was buried under the quilt, and when he heard the squeak, his little hands tentatively lowered the quilt so he could peep at her.

"Hi, Bobby. How are you doing?"

"I want my mummy," he cried, sniffing.

Kayli entered the room and approached the bed. She eased herself down beside him and stroked his tiny fingers. "I know, sweetie. She won't be long. Hey, I've rung Nanny. She's sending Granddad to come and collect us. That'll be fun, won't it?"

Instead of Bobby leaping out of bed in an excited haze, his sobbing increased, and he buried his head fully beneath the quilt. Defeated, Kayli wandered around the room and opened the wardrobe door. At the bottom, she found a small rucksack. She bent down to retrieve it and placed the two bedtime storybooks inside. Then she looked on the back of the door for Bobby's dressing gown. She found a red towelling robe and a Winnie the Pooh gown. Kayli unhooked the towelling robe from the door and tried again to coax Bobby out from beneath the covers.

"Come on, Bobby, we need to get a wriggle on. Granddad will be here soon."

Again, his sobbing increased. Kayli chanced her arm and sat on the edge of his bed. She remained silent until his crying subsided. He had moved his whole body to the opposite side of the bed and was teetering on the edge, trying to get away from her. She didn't have a clue what to say or how to react to get her nephew to respond positively towards her.

Around fifteen minutes later, the doorbell rang. "Ooo... I wonder who that could be. Want to come with me and have a look?"

Two tiny hands appeared and pulled the cover down to reveal his tear-stained pink face. Her heart almost broke in two when she saw him. She jumped off the bed, gathered his things and ran down the stairs, hoping that Bobby would be intrigued enough to follow her.

Kayli let out a relieved breath when she opened the front door to find her father standing there. She flew into his arms, tears of frustration and concern for Annabelle welling up in her eyes. "Oh, Dad, I feel such a failure."

Her father smoothed her hair down and whispered, "There, there, dear. The cavalry has arrived now. We'll soon get the little man responding. Dry your eyes. This isn't like you." He pushed her away from him and withdrew a clean white cotton hanky from his jacket pocket before he stepped through the front door.

Kayli dried her eyes on the hanky and sighed heavily. "Can you try and get him down, Dad? Even telling him that you were on your way over here didn't have the desired impact I had hoped for. The poor chap is broken-hearted up there."

"I'll go and sort him out. Are you ready to go?"

"Yes. I just need to find his shoes, and we can get off." Kayli's gaze rose to the top of the stairs. Bobby had his left hand resting on the bannister, and in his right hand, he was holding his favourite teddy bear. He was staring down at them, looking slightly confused. Kayli took a step towards the stairs, but her father grabbed her arm.

"Leave him to me, love," he whispered. Then he smiled up at Bobby and held out a hand to him. "Come on, Bobby. Shall we go and see what Grandma has got for you? I think she mentioned having some cheesecake in the fridge. Now what kind was it again? Oh yes, I think it was strawberry. That's your favourite, isn't it, son?"

Bobby placed his teddy bear up to his mouth and sucked on one of its paws, nodding slowly.

Kayli's father held out a hand to him. "Quickly then. We better get over there before Grandma decides to give the cheesecake to the birds."

Bobby descended the stairs slowly, unsure of his footing at times, until he reached the bottom. Kayli threw the towelling robe around his shoulders and slotted his arms through the sleeves, then she helped him slip on a pair of Thomas the Tank Engine slippers she'd found underneath the stairs.

"We're ready to leave now, Dad. I'll just grab my handbag." She fetched her bag from the lounge and picked up the rucksack.

Bobby was eyeing her suspiciously as he gripped his grandfather's hand tightly. Her father whisked Bobby up into his arms and snuggled his nose into the boy's neck, making him chuckle. It was wonderful to see the child happy again. She'd always known that she would make a lousy mother, but that night's ghastly experience had only reinforced that idea.

"I'll follow you in my car, if that's okay?"

"Of course. I'll secure the little man in the back seat, and we'll hit the road."

Kayli pulled the front door to behind her and tested it to make sure it was locked, then she helped her father place Bobby in his special seat before she jumped in her own car.

She followed her father's car back to his house, and halfway through the journey, her phone rang. She answered it on the hands-free device. "Hello, is that you, Mark?"

"You sound distant. Where are you?"

"It's a long story. I'm on my way to my parents' house. Is everything all right with you?"

"Yep, fine. Just calling to say I think I'm going to like it here, love. Why are you going to your parents' house?"

Kayli's heart sank when he told her he was going to enjoy his job. "Annabelle got rushed into hospital. Giles rang me to look after Bobby, but he was freaking out and was crying for his mum. I tried consoling him, but it was hopeless. In the end, I rang Mum for advice, and she sent Dad over to get us."

"Crap! Is Annabelle all right?"

"They think it's the baby, love. We'll know more later."

"Damn, send them both my best wishes the next time you speak to Giles."

"I will. Glad you're enjoying your job. I've got to go, love. See you later. Don't be surprised if I'm not there when you get home."

"No problem. I'm not likely to think you've run out on me. You love me too much to do that."

"I'm glad you realise that. Speak later. Love you."

"Take care. Love to everyone." Mark ended the call.

The rest of the journey consisted of Kayli feeling tormented, not only concerned for Annabelle's welfare, but also worried about whether Mark had truly meant what he'd said about enjoying his job. She hoped not. *What kind of married life will we have, not seeing each other?*

Sometimes she didn't get home from work until around seven, and his shift was due to start around eight. She slammed the heel of her hand into the steering wheel, and the judder rippled up her arm and through her body. *Something needs to change. Either I need to jack in my job, or Mark needs to find a nine-to-five job.* She made a mental note to have a word with her father once Bobby was tucked up in bed.

~ ~ ~

Ten minutes later, they arrived at her parents' house. Her mother was waiting on the doorstep, looking frozen. "Go in, Mum. You'll catch your death!"

"I'm fine. How's Bobby? Has he settled down now?"

Kayli held open the car's back door while her father unfastened the little man from his seat and swept him into his arms. "He's fine. I'll just get his bag."

Her mother stepped behind the front door to allow them in. "Hello, Bobby. It's lovely to see you. Are you tired?"

The wide-eyed Bobby glanced between the three of them, still looking mightily confused.

"He's looking forward to having some of his grandmother's cheesecake," Kayli's father said.

Her mother winked at Kayli. "Oh, I see. Well, we'll have to see what we can find in the fridge, then, won't we?"

Her father set the wriggling Bobby on the floor in the hallway, and he slipped his hand into his grandmother's outstretched hand.

Kayli exhaled a relieved sigh as her mother led Bobby into the kitchen. "You guys are brilliant with him. Giles must have been out of his mind thinking that I could cope on my own with the little munchkin. Thanks, Dad." She hugged her father and pecked him on the cheek. "Can we have a chat later? Once Bobby is settled in bed?"

"Of course. Is something bothering you, apart from the Annabelle situation?"

"Yes and no. Let's sort Bobby out first then chat."

She followed her father into the kitchen, where they found a smiling Bobby tucking into a medium-sized portion of her mother's homemade cheesecake. There was another larger portion sitting on the worktop.

"Does that piece have my name on it?" Kayli asked hopefully.

"It does. Would you like a nice cup of fresh coffee to go with it?" her mother asked.

"You read my mind. Not sure what I would have done without your help tonight."

"These things are sent to try us, love. It's all good now... well, not quite, but you get my drift." Her mother ruffled Bobby's hair. "Eat up, little one. Is it nice?"

His eyes sparkled, and he nodded enthusiastically as he guided a heaped teaspoonful into his gaping mouth.

With Bobby less stressed out, Kayli's thoughts shifted to Annabelle and Giles. She was tempted to ring her brother to see how things were going, but she knew that was a bad idea so soon.

Once Bobby had finished his glass of milk and licked the plate clean of his cheesecake, he willingly kissed everyone goodnight and left the room with his grandmother.

"His bedtime stories are in the rucksack at the bottom of the stairs, Mum," Kayli called out.

Her father chuckled. "My guess is that little boy will be sound asleep within minutes after eating that huge dessert. He seemed to enjoy it, bless him."

"He did. It must have been so confusing for him to wake up and find me there in his room."

"I think it would unsettle me too," her father joked. "Anyway, what did you want to talk to me about? Something that you'd rather keep from your mother?"

"Not really. You know how much I hate secrets."

Her father raised his eyebrows, and she flinched.

"Okay, maybe that was silly, me saying that after keeping you both out of the loop while Giles and I took off on our travels."

"You could say that. I take it this little chat is about the job I found for Mark. Am I right?"

Kayli inhaled a large breath and let it out slowly before she replied, "I'm really grateful, Dad. I don't want this to sound as if I'm not, but heck! A bouncer at a nightclub?"

"It's an honest day's job, love. What's wrong with it? Has Mark complained?"

Her cheeks warmed under his gaze. "No. If you must know, he rang me on the way over here and said he thought he was going to enjoy his new job."

"So where does the problem lie, then? With you?"

Her gaze dropped to the table. "Maybe it's me being selfish… I don't know. Put yourself in my shoes. I usually get home around six thirty, sometimes seven thirty, depending on how my day has gone and what the traffic is like on the way home. That means I'll get little time with Mark before he has to leave for work. We'll be on opposite shifts all the time. Not only that, when he comes in at three or four in the morning, you can be sure my sleep will get disturbed. He's like an elephant stomping around the bedroom when he gets up to have a wee during the night."

Her father laughed. "I really don't want to know the ins and outs of your husband's nightly bathroom routine, love."

"Sorry. I was simply sharing how I envisage things playing out when he gets home at all hours. You know what I'm like if I don't get my eight hours' sleep. I need all my concentration for work. It's going to be hard getting back to sleep once he comes home from work."

"I think you're blowing things out of proportion, darling. Why don't you give it a week to see how things pan out? Perhaps you can start going to bed earlier."

"Why should I alter my routine to fit in with his new job?"

"Marriage is all about compromises, Kayli. You have a lot to learn if you haven't figured that one out by now."

Kayli twisted her mug of coffee on the table until her father placed his hand over hers. "Sorry. I suppose you're right. Will you do me a favour, though, Dad?"

He tilted his head. "What's that, love?"

"Keep your eye open for another job for him, maybe one that coincides with my shifts."

"I'll do my best for you both. Although this time next year, I bet you'll be begging me to find him a job on the other side of the world again."

Kayli laughed and shook her head. "No way! I never want him stepping foot outside the country again, not unless it's with me on a holiday."

"I can understand that, love."

Kayli's mother entered the room, looking as if she had the weight of the world on her shoulders. "Everything all right, Mum?"

"With Bobby, yes. He went straight off before I'd even read half a page to him. It's Annabelle I'm concerned about. What if she loses the baby?"

A dark cloud appeared to descend on the room. "I know. I keep thinking the same. I feel so guilty too."

"Why on earth should you feel guilty, love?" her mother demanded, reaching for Kayli's hand.

"If I hadn't dragged Giles out to Afghanistan with me, the baby probably would be all right now."

Her mother shook her head adamantly. "That's you being daft. This has nothing to do with that, Kayli. From day one, Annabelle has been unwell during her pregnancy. Sometimes we have to listen to our bodies. Not all babies go full term. If she loses it, then there must have been something wrong with the child. The body sometimes rejects something that doesn't feel right. Maybe it's for the best."

She had never heard her mother talk that way before. *How could she be so dismissive of the child Annabelle was carrying?* Searching her mother's eyes, she discovered a pain lurking there that she'd never noticed before.

"What are you trying to say, Mum? Has this happened to you?"

A sad look passed between her mother and her father.

Kayli slumped back in her chair, devastated for her parents. "When?"

Large tears brimmed in her mother's eyes before one fell onto her right cheek. She swiped it away. "Years ago. Actually, it was between you and Giles. I was sick from the get-go with that child. I lost the baby before the twelve weeks."

Kayli gasped. "I'm so sorry. Why didn't you tell us?"

Her mother shrugged. "Your father and I thought it would be better to move on with our lives and promised that we would never look back in any form of regret. We had you and your brother, so we were lucky. Some people out there aren't that fortunate, love. They go through miscarriage after miscarriage, hoping to hold a baby in their arms, without success. Let's not discuss this until we know for certain what the prognosis is."

"Annabelle seemed pretty sure that she'd lost it, Mum. She was as white as a sheet when I arrived."

"That doesn't sound good, then. They'll both need our support over the coming weeks."

The three of them sat there in silence for the next twenty minutes, until Kayli's phone rang. The caller ID told her it was her brother ringing. She swallowed then answered. "Hello, Giles, any news?"

"It's gone, Kayli. Annabelle has lost the baby."

"No! Oh, Giles, I'm so sorry. I don't know what to say other than that. My heart goes out to you both. I'm at Mum and Dad's. Let me put Mum on."

"What? Why? Where's Bobby?" he asked frantically.

"He's here. Bobby woke up inconsolable, and I couldn't settle him down, so I had to call in reinforcements. Do you want me to come to the hospital to be with you?"

"I see. Is Bobby all right now? No, don't come here. Annabelle has been given a sedative, and she's sleepy now."

"Bobby is sound asleep. I'll put the phone on speaker." Kayli nodded for her mother to speak to him.

"Hello, dear. Your father and I are so sorry. Is Annabelle all right?"

Her brother broke down in tears. "We're both devastated, Mum. I'm not sure she'll get over this. I know we didn't plan this pregnancy, but in the last few weeks, she's been making plans to decorate the nursery again."

"It'll be hard for her to cope to begin with, darling. Of course it will. Just remain strong for her, as she'll be relying on you more than ever to say the right things when she needs to hear them." Kayli's mother reached across the table and grasped her father's hands until her knuckles turned white.

"I know, Mum. I'll always be there for her... at least I will be from now on."

Kayli flinched. Is he referring to our trip? I know I'd feel bitter about it if I were in his shoes. I'm feeling enough guilt for both of us at the moment as it is. If only I hadn't forced his hand into coming with me, perhaps the baby would have survived. Tears dripped onto her cheek.

"Send Annabelle our love and give her a gentle hug from us. Keep us informed, son. We love you both."

"I will. Speak to you later." Giles hung up without saying he loved his mother back, and that was unheard of from him.

Kayli broke down in tears. "This is down to me and my selfish behaviour. If I hadn't forced Giles to go out there with me, this wouldn't have happened," she mumbled through the sobs.

Her mother left her chair and pulled Kayli to her feet. She hugged her gently and whispered, "This isn't like you, love. You mustn't blame yourself. These things happen from time to time, and no one knows why. But it's certainly not because of any stress you might have caused Annabelle. You must get that out of your head. Do you hear me?"

Sniffling, Kayli dried her eyes on the sleeve of her jacket and gazed into her mother's tearful eyes. "I know you're only saying this to make me feel better, and it's not going to shift either the guilt or the hurt that are tearing me apart inside, Mum."

"That hurt and guilt will dissipate over time. I promise you."

"Your mother is right, Kayli. No one is going to blame you for this, not even Giles and Annabelle. You mark my words on that one. They may be a bit different once they're home, only because they'll be grieving the little one, but you mustn't take that personally. You hear me?"

"It's a little hard not to take all of this personally, Dad, when Mark and I were at the centre of the problem in the first place."

"Just give it time. Listen to me. If either Giles or Annabelle blamed you in any way, do you really think you would be the first person they rang to look after Bobby? No, they wouldn't. Now stop being silly. Grieve for the baby like all of us but don't allow that grief to be tinged with guilt."

Kayli's gaze drifted between her parents, who shared another secret look between them. "I can't promise. I'll definitely try my best, though."

Her mother kissed her on the cheek. "Good girl. Look, why don't I make up a spare bed for you, so you can stay the night here with us?"

"That's kind, Mum. I think I'd rather go home, if it's all the same to you. Shall I take Bobby with me?"

"No, he's better off staying put here. He's asleep now, and it seems a shame to disturb him."

"Would you mind if I go home? It's been a trying day."

Her mother shook her head and brushed away Kayli's tears. "You go. You've had a shock. Everything will look much clearer in a few days, love."

"I hope you're right, Mum. Thanks for understanding. I'm sorry you've experienced the same loss and grief over the years as Giles and Annabelle are going through right now."

Her mother shrugged. "It's called life, love. The terrible traumas we go through make us stronger. You of all people should understand that after your recent adventure."

"I do. We have to grasp each day and treat it as a gift. If you're sure about Bobby, I'll set off, then. I'll ring Giles when I get home, make him aware of the situation. Thank you both. We'd be lost without you guys to fall back on."

Her father stepped forward to hug her. "That's what family are for, to call on each other when help is needed. Go home and get some rest."

Kayli sprinted upstairs to poke her head in the spare room to see if Bobby was still asleep. A gentle snore was coming from his bed, and he had his head tucked under the quilt. She smiled and went downstairs again. "He's sound asleep. I'll ring you in the morning. Love you both, and thank you again for being the best parents in the world."

The three of them shared a group hug before Kayli left the house. She waved at her mum and dad then left the drive. She was distracted by her dark, gloomy thoughts all the way home. She parked in a space close to her house and locked the car.

Kayli had time to pour herself a much-needed glass of red wine before her phone rang. It was Mark. "Hello, you. How are things going there?"

"Really well. It's just a quick one to see how things are with Giles and Annabelle."

"Not good. They lost the baby."

"Shit! That's bad luck. I was wondering if it had anything to do with the stress we put them through a few weeks ago."

"I'm glad we're on the same wavelength. Mum and Dad assured me that I'm daft to think that way. Things like this happen more often than we think, according to Mum, who revealed she had a miscarriage herself years ago."

"What? And she didn't tell you?"

"No. Hey, we'll talk about it later. You better go."

"Yep, I hear you. I'm getting the evil eye here."

"See you later."

"Kayli, keep your chin up. I love you. They'll get through this. I promise you."

"I hope so." Kayli ended the call and sat on the sofa in the dark for the next few hours, revisiting the dangers they had endured in the past month or so and the subsequent consequences of their actions.

She must have drifted off to sleep, because the next thing she knew, Mark was lifting her in his arms and carrying her up to bed.

"What time is it?" she asked sleepily.

"Almost three thirty, my sleeping beauty."

He placed her gently on the bed, and she didn't remember anything else until her alarm went off at seven. The noise confused her at first. Mark reached across her and hit the clock with his fist. He hovered over her and looked down, sweeping back the hair covering her face.

"How are you feeling?" he asked, brushing his lips against hers.

"Like my head and my body belong to someone else. Crap, are we really going to be able to cope with our shift patterns being opposite to each other?"

"We will. We'll get used to it."

She pulled back the quilt to find herself still fully clothed. "Shit! I'll have to send this suit to the cleaners now."

"I didn't have the heart to disturb you more than necessary last night."

"No problem. Try and go back to sleep. I'll have a quick shower and shoot off. I'll get changed in the spare room so I don't make any unnecessary noise."

"I'm fine. I can sleep anywhere at any time. It's you I'm worried about."

"Well, don't. We'll get through this. It's a minor inconvenience compared to what some people are going through."

"You're right." He kissed her then rolled over. "See you later. Ring me during the day if you get the chance."

"I will. Sleep well."

CHAPTER EIGHT

The team were already hard at work when Kayli entered the incident room.

"Crikey, you look like death warmed up. Heavy night on the vino with your mates last night?" Dave quipped as soon as he laid eyes on her.

Kayli glared at him and shook her head. "If you must know, there was a death in the family last night." Her tone was much harsher than she'd intended, and as soon as the words left her lips, she regretted saying them. "Sorry, that was uncalled for. Let me have a coffee, and I'll explain later."

"I'm sorry. I had no idea," Dave mumbled.

She passed his desk on the way to the vending machine and touched his shoulder. "I shouldn't have snapped like that. It should be me dishing out the apologies."

Kayli bought a coffee and slipped into her office, anything to avoid the looks of sympathy emanating from her team. *Damn, yet more guilt to add to the amount I'm already carrying on my shoulders.*

She buried herself in paperwork for the next hour or so until Dave poked his head into the room.

"Come in and take a seat."

"I just wanted to apologise for my cock-up earlier."

Kayli smiled. "No need. You couldn't have known." She sighed and leaned back in her chair. "Annabelle lost the baby last night."

"No, that's rough. I'm so sorry. Were you at the hospital until all hours?"

"No. Giles rang me to look after Bobby while he went to the hospital with Annabelle. I suck at babysitting kids. Bobby woke up and was broken-hearted to find his parents weren't there. I panicked and called my mum and dad. Dad came to fetch him, and Bobby slept there the night. Damn, I should have rung them first thing to see how he is."

Dave struggled to stand and walked towards the door. "I'll leave you to it."

"I appreciate that, Dave. I'll be out shortly." As soon as her partner left the room, she dialled her parents' number. "Hi, Mum. Just checking in on the little man. Is he up and about yet?"

"Hello, darling. Oh yes, he was up and jumping around on his bed at six o'clock this morning. Your father has taken him to the park for a kick around. Giles came by this morning to drop off a change of clothes for Bobby."

"He did? How was he?"

"He looked shell-shocked, as he's bound to. They'll survive this. Don't you fret. How are you feeling this morning?"

"Like I went ten rounds with Amir Khan."

Her mother chuckled. "Only the ten rounds? I was going to say don't beat yourself up over this, Kayli, but it seems inappropriate after your comment. Are you at work?"

"Oh, yes. I couldn't sit at home, stewing over things. Do you think I should ring Giles? Or should I wait until he contacts me?"

"I think you're making too much of this, love. He was fine when he came to visit Bobby earlier. Well, not fine, but he's accepted the situation for what it is."

"I'll give him a ring this afternoon, then. Did he say how long Annabelle was expected to stay in hospital?"

"Another day or so. There are procedures they need to carry out before they let her come home. I won't bore you with the gruesome details."

"I don't profess to know what you're talking about, and I'm not sure I want to know what those procedures are. Poor Annabelle."

"Giles said they'll be making plans for the funeral in the next day or so."

Kayli gasped. "Oh, Lordy, that's another aspect I hadn't thought about."

"It's different nowadays to when I lost the baby. Anyway, enough about that. I must go, darling. I have a cake in the oven."

"Okay, thanks for the update, Mum. Take care. I'll be in touch soon."

Before Kayli could replace the phone in its docking station, there was a knock on the door. "Come in."

Graeme rushed into the room, his eyes wide with excitement. "We've located the car, boss."

"Paul Potts's car?"

"Yes, it's just over the border in South Wales."

"And? Was he in the car?"

"That information is unknown at present as the car is in a deep ravine. They've called in the mountain rescue team to get the car out of there as it's difficult to get a fire engine into the area."

"Really? Okay, Dave and I better get over there ASAP. Get the postcode for me for the satnav, Graeme. Good work locating it."

"I just put the feelers out, boss." He left the office.

Kayli tidied her paperwork away and removed her jacket from the back of her chair. She joined her partner at the door to the incident room. "Have you got the directions we need?"

Dave waved the slip of paper. "I have. Should only take us an hour or so to get there, depending on the traffic, of course."

"Brilliant. Let's do this."

~ ~ ~

It took them an hour and a half in the end to find the correct location as Kayli took the decision to avoid the toll road over the Severn Bridge. The road was tight and winding, quite high up compared to the other roads in the area.

Dave pointed to some vehicles parked in a slight clearing. "Looks like this is the spot we're after."

Kayli drew up alongside a Land Rover. "Do you want to stay here? I don't think the ground looks very safe for someone on crutches."

"If I have to," Dave grumbled.

"I'll see how it goes underfoot and give you the signal for you to join me if I think it's suitable. How's that?"

"Fair enough."

Kayli hopped out and went to the boot of her car. She withdrew a pair of Wellington boots and slipped them on, then she trudged up the muddy bank to where a group of men, some in uniform, others in rescue gear, were standing. "Hi. I'm DI Kayli Bright of the Avon and Somerset Constabulary. I believe you've found a car that we've been searching for."

A uniformed officer came towards her with an outstretched hand. "I placed the call, ma'am. Constable Edwards," he said with a slight Welsh lilt. "We were informed to keep an eye out for the vehicle and report back to your team."

"Thanks for contacting us. Now, what do we have?"

"The car is at the bottom, ma'am. The mountain rescue team are going to have to winch it out of the river."

Kayli stretched out a little and looked over the edge at the car below, which was lying flat on the riverbed, half-immersed in the fast-flowing water. "Who found the car?"

"A couple of walkers, ma'am. I've taken a statement from them and sent them on their way. I hope that was okay?"

"Of course. I bet they were shaken up."

"They were. Two women, it was. I've also placed a call to the local pathologist. He sent his team ahead, and they're over there, ma'am, if you want to have a word with them."

"Thanks. I'll do that." Kayli smiled at the constable then squelched through the mud towards the two men wearing white suits. "Hi. I'm Kayli Bright, the SIO on the case. I take it they're getting ready to winch the car up. Is it all right to do that without the pathologist being here?"

"In such a dangerous position, yes, it's fine. The pathologist wouldn't put his life in danger going down such a steep slope."

"Is he going to be long?"

"Around half an hour. He was dealing with a fatal crash a few miles away."

"We're about to winch her up now, guys. Stand back, just in case anything should go wrong," a burly rescue team member said.

Kayli shuffled to stand alongside the forensics technicians as the three members of the rescue team manned the winch and guided the car up the steep incline.

"Whoa! It's going to snag on the overhanging branch," a team member shouted. He searched around him and picked up a long branch lying on the ground. He pointed it down the bank to pin back the branch blocking the car's path. "Okay, it's safe to continue now."

The winch started up again, and the car inched its way closer to them, water pouring from the door seals.

Kayli heard a rustle behind her, and she turned swiftly to find Dave huffing after his exertion to be with her. "You should have stayed in the car. It's far too dangerous for you."

"It's muddy. Not too bad. The crutches didn't sink in far. I kept to the undergrowth. I'll keep away from the edge," he said, straining his neck to look at the car.

Kayli gripped his arm so he could have a better view. "Not sure what we're going to find inside."

"The amount of water still coming out of the doors, I wouldn't hold on to any hope of him being still alive if he's in there."

"I think I'd come to that conclusion myself, partner."

He grinned sheepishly and mumbled an apology.

Within minutes, the car had ascended the incline, and the rescue team were winching it onto a secure flat area close by.

Kayli stepped towards the car tentatively. "All right if I have a look inside?" she asked the rescue team and the men from forensics.

"Just be careful."

"That goes without saying." Kayli slipped on a pair of latex gloves and approached the driver's door. Peering through the mucky window, she struggled to make out if there was anything inside the vehicle. She eased the door open, and yet more water poured out. Once the small waterfall had died down, she took a step forward for a closer inspection.

"Anything?" Dave asked impatiently from behind her.

"Give me a chance. Nope, I can't see anything in the front or the back. How strange."

"Which probably means that he dumped the car and made his way away from here on foot."

Kayli stood back and shrugged. "Maybe he was being followed and someone was waiting for him on the road while he dumped the car."

"Perplexing either way. Then there's the issue of Bob Nuttall to consider in this scenario," Dave said.

"Maybe he was the one waiting for him. We need to get on to Graeme and tell him to focus on what else was going on with Potts's car. Was he being followed here?"

While they were discussing the possibilities of what had happened, one of the forensics team opened the boot of the car and called over, "You might want to rethink all of that, Inspector."

Kayli rushed towards the boot and stared down at a man's lifeless body. "Damn."

Kayli heard a car pull up and turned to see a man in his fifties trudging through the muddy area towards them.

He extended his hand to Kayli. "I'm the pathologist, Greg Hughes."

"Hi. I'm the SIO in charge of the case, DI Kayli Bright, and this is my partner, DS Dave Chaplin. It's not good news. We've found the owner of the vehicle—he's the person who was reported missing—in the boot of the car."

"That's a shame. Let me examine the body and see if I can at least give you a cause of death."

"I'm surmising that he couldn't have done this himself. There's no way he could have hidden in the boot and driven the car over the edge at the same time."

"That would be my probable assumption from the outset," Greg said. "May I?"

Kayli stepped back to allow him access to the vehicle. She held out her hand to hold his case for him rather than letting him place it in the nearby mud.

"Hmm… my initial assessment would say that the victim drowned."

Kayli glanced at her partner then looked back at the pathologist. "You're saying you think he was still alive when he went over the edge?"

"I believe so." He moved the victim's head slightly and pulled it forward. "He has an open wound on the back of his head."

"Are you thinking someone whacked him from behind?" Kayli asked.

The pathologist nodded as he continued his assessment. "The space is confined, too confined for me to give you anything else at this time, Inspector. I would say that the victim was bludgeoned with a blunt object and shoved in the boot of the car, then someone either pushed the car over the edge, or more likely, drove the car and jumped out of the vehicle at the last minute before its journey into the ravine could gain momentum. I'll know more once the post-mortem has been performed. I'll send you my report as soon as possible."

"Thanks. I'd appreciate that. I don't suppose you can establish the time of death?"

"Not at this moment in time. It'll be in my report," Greg added abruptly.

Kayli could tell he was eager to get the body moved and back to the lab. "Thank you. We'll leave you to it. We'll visit the family members to let them know Mr. Potts has been found."

He nodded and turned his back to dismiss her. As Kayli and Dave trudged through the mud back to the car, she heard the pathologist giving his men instructions.

"Is that where we're heading now? To tell the family?" Dave asked as Kayli handed him a small hand towel for him to wipe the mud from the bottom of his crutches before he entered the car.

"Yep. I think we should tell Anita first, but it was her uncle who made the initial contact with us."

"Maybe call him and ask him to be at the house when you break the news to Anita. I'm guessing she's going to need his support. She seemed a little fragile to me when we visited her."

"You're right." Kayli withdrew her phone from her pocket and rang the station. "Hi, Donna. We've located Paul Potts's body inside the boot of the car."

"Oh no. That's dreadful. I'll let Graeme know."

"Okay. What I need is Samuel Potts's phone number, if you will?"

Donna reeled off the number, and Kayli memorised it. "We'll be back soon. Thanks, Donna." She dialled Samuel's number and leaned against the car while she waited for him to answer.

"Hello."

"Hello, Mr. Potts. This is DI Kayli Bright. I have some news regarding your brother and wondered if you would meet me at his house in about an hour."

"You've found him? Is he all right? Are you bringing him home, Inspector?"

"Sorry, sir. Yes, we've found your brother, but it's not good news, I'm afraid. We're on our way to let his daughter know and thought you could be there to support her. I have a feeling the news will come as a blow to her, and to you, of course."

"Oh no! I can't believe he's gone. Can you give me any more details? On second thoughts, I don't think I want to know. I'll make my way over to be with Anita now."

"Thank you. I really appreciate that. See you soon."

Kayli ended the call and walked around the other side of the car to relieve Dave of the muddy towel. She held open the door for him to swing his legs into the passenger seat before she flung the towel and her muddy wellies into the boot. The journey back across the border was a quiet one, each of the detectives lost in thought about the case.

They pulled up outside Paul Potts's home just over an hour later. Samuel was waiting at the door for them, his face ashen. Kayli shook his hand. "Good to see you again, sir. I'm sorry for your loss. Is Anita home?"

"Yes, she's here. I haven't said anything. However, I do think she knows something is wrong. Come in. Can I get you both a coffee?"

Kayli shook her head. "We're fine, thank you."

"Go through to the lounge. Anita is in there."

Kayli led the way and eased open the door to find a terrified Anita staring back at her. "Hello, Anita. Can we come in?"

The young woman jumped out of her chair and wiped her hand on her jeans before extending it. Kayli clutched her hand and smiled at her.

"Take a seat," Anita said.

Kayli and Dave dropped onto the sofa while Samuel chose to stand alongside his niece as she lowered herself into her father's armchair.

Kayli sighed and looked Anita in the eye. "I'm sorry, Anita, but I'm afraid your father's body was discovered this morning."

Anita screamed and buried her face in her hands.

Samuel placed a comforting arm around his niece's shoulders and asked, "Where?"

"His car was found in a deep ravine just over the border in South Wales."

"Was it an accident? Did he drive off the road?"

Kayli shook her head. "No. It wasn't an accident. We believe your brother was murdered when his car was pushed into the gorge."

Samuel's legs gave way, and he sank onto the arm of the chair his niece was sitting in and stared open-mouthed at Kayli. Anita began to rock back and forth, unable to prevent the tears cascading down her cheeks.

"I'm so sorry. There was no easy way to tell you. A post-mortem will be carried out either today or tomorrow, and it will determine the cause of death, but the pathologist's initial assessment was that Paul was bludgeoned over the head before he was thrown into the boot of his car."

"And that's what killed him? The blow to the head?" Samuel asked, shaking his head in disbelief.

"The pathologist believes he drowned."

Anita wailed again. Kayli's heart went out to the young woman. The thought of losing her own father in such a grotesque manner was very hard to fathom.

Anita dropped her hands from her face. She sniffed and raised her head to look at her uncle. "Why? Why would anyone kill him? He's such a gentle man. Showed people only kindness. Who would want to kill him? For what reason? I can't believe it. Not my father. I'll never see him again." She broke down again.

Samuel pulled her towards him, resting her head against his chest. "It's beyond me, love. I'm sure the inspector and her team will be doing their utmost to find the person. Do you have any suspects, Inspector?"

"Maybe. We're not sure just yet. One of the tenants at the flats used the fire escape rather than speak to us on Monday, and we've been trying to track him down ever since."

"You think he did this? Which one? Not that I know all of their names," Samuel said.

"Bob Nuttall. He rented the flat at the top of the house. I'm sure it's only a matter of time before we catch up with him. Do you recall your brother ever mentioning his name in connection to anything? An argument he'd had with him, perhaps?"

Anita sniffled and nodded. "Dad was annoyed with him about not paying the rent. He told me that if Nuttall didn't pay what he owed by the end of the week, he was going to kick him out. Would that be enough for someone to react like that and kill my father?" she said, her voice strained with emotion.

"The slightest thing can spark a person's anger gene to explode." Kayli didn't feel the need to share with either of them about the vast sum of money they had discovered in Nuttall's flat.

"Why, though? If it is him. Why would he deliberately set out to kill Paul?"

Kayli shrugged. "That's what we'll be asking Nuttall when we find him. Not only that—why drive all the way to Wales to get rid of your brother's body?"

"Let's hope you find this man soon," Samuel said, hugging Anita to him.

Kayli rose from her seat, and Dave hoisted himself to his feet. "We'll get back to the station now. I wanted to drop by and tell you in person and to assure you that we'll be doing everything we can to find the person responsible in the hope of bringing them to justice. Will you pass on our condolences to Sharon and Dylan?"

Anita glanced up and nodded. "I'll get Uncle Samuel to ring them after you've gone."

Samuel walked across the room and opened the door.

"Thanks. Take care of yourself, Anita. I'm deeply sorry for your loss," Kayli said before she and Dave left the room. She shook Samuel's hand at the front door. "You have my deepest sympathy, Samuel. Thank you for being here today."

"It should be me thanking you, Inspector. At least you've managed to find my brother's body before... well, you know what I mean... before it had a chance to deteriorate."

"I'll be in touch with you again as soon as I have any more news for you. Take care."

He shook Dave's hand and closed the door behind them.

"Crap! I hate breaking news like that, especially to a nice family such as this," Dave said.

Kayli pressed the key fob to unlock the doors. "Good job you didn't have to do it, then." She grinned at her partner over the roof of the car before she slipped into the driver's seat.

Dave made a face at her once he was settled in his seat. "You know what I meant. What now?"

"I think I'm going to call a press conference. Let's rock Nuttall's boat and plaster his picture all over the media."

"Good idea. Can I ask why you haven't done it before?"

Kayli started the engine. "Maybe I just needed confirmation that Potts hadn't just decided to take off somewhere for some peace and quiet. You know what the statistics are for the number of people who go missing simply as an excuse to get away from family members."

"I've got a rough idea. Let's hope something comes of the appeal. Nuttall clearly doesn't have any cash on him. Otherwise, he would have topped up his car, so that limits the places he can doss down, right?"

"I was thinking along the same lines. Mind you, he could be hiding out at a mate's house."

"True."

CHAPTER NINE

Kayli called in a bunch of favours to get the media on board with the appeal. Contacts from both the local paper and the local TV stations joined her in the conference suite at the station at four o'clock that afternoon. Armed with her notes and a mugshot of Bob Nuttall, Kayli settled herself at the long table as the cameras rolled.

"Thank you for attending today and at such short notice. On Monday of this week, a call came in to me that a local man had gone missing. Since then, my team and I have been trying to find out what happened to Paul Potts. He was the landlord of a house in the Clifton area of Bristol. When we called at the flats to question the tenants, one person in particular"—Kayli held up the mugshot of Nuttall for the cameras—"absconded from his flat. This man is Bob Nuttall. We've been trying to trace him ever since. Can you help us? He was driving a dark blue Opel Manta at the time. We've since located the car, and Bob Nuttall was spotted on nearby CCTV cameras leaving the scene, heading into the city. Have you seen this man?"

Kayli glanced around the sea of media faces staring back at her. "Any questions?"

One keen young journalist raised his hand. "Patrick Knowles of the Bristol Evening News. Can you tell us why you're involved in this case? Aren't you a murder-squad detective?"

Kayli smiled at the young man, who had obviously carried out his research well. "I am. Unfortunately, as of this morning, the missing persons case has been upgraded to a murder enquiry following the discovery of Mr. Potts's body."

"Can I ask where and how the victim died?" Mr. Knowles asked.

"As to how he died, I'm not at liberty to say until the post-mortem has been carried out. Mr. Potts's vehicle was found in a ravine in South Wales. That's as much as I'm able to share with you all right now. This is why it's imperative that we locate Bob Nuttall. Any more questions?"

A few of the journalists raised their hands, and Kayli pointed to a young woman. "Yes?"

"Cassandra Watt from BBC News. Inspector, do you have any other suspects in mind, or is Bob Nuttall your prime suspect on this case?"

"At this point, he is indeed our prime suspect. Why run unless he has something to hide? Anyone else have any other questions?"

A few more hands went up. Kayli pointed to an older woman with striking red hair. "Yes, Melody?"

The woman nodded in acknowledgement. "Does this person you're seeking have a motive, Inspector?"

"I'd rather keep that side of things under wraps for now. All I need to do is to establish Bob Nuttall's whereabouts so that he can be brought in for questioning." Kayli held the man's picture up again. "Have you seen this man in your area in the last few days? If you have, please call the number at the bottom of your screen. It's imperative that we speak to him as soon as possible." Kayli received the thumbs-up that the camera had stopped rolling, and she drew the appeal to a close. "Thank you for your prompt cooperation on this matter, ladies and gentlemen. As always, it's truly appreciated. Now if you'll excuse me, I have a killer to catch."

Kayli made her way back up to the incident room on heavy, weary legs. It had already been a long day, and if the public felt like being super informative, she figured she would still be at the station well into the evening. The team were all sitting at their desks, primed, ready to pounce on the phones once they started ringing. "Out of our hands now, guys. All we can do is do a Sidney Youngblood."

Dave's face twisted into a look of confusion. "Is that supposed to mean something?"

Kayli placed an embarrassed hand over her face and shook her head. "Crap! I can't believe I said that out loud. It's a family joke. Giles and I used to love his top-ten hit when we were kids. Don't tell me you've never heard of 'Sit and Wait'?"

Dave shrugged and glanced at the others. "Nope. Anyone else?"

Donna's mouth turned down at the sides. "Can't say I have."

Graeme, on the other hand, was nodding and smiling. "I only know it through Lindy. She mentioned you and Giles used to say it all the time."

"True. Sorry for the confusion, team."

Graeme gestured with a raised finger that he would like to speak. Kayli nodded for him to go ahead. "While you were doing the appeal, boss, I took the liberty of ringing a couple of my contacts on the street. I hope that was okay?"

"Of course it was. And?"

"Nothing known as yet. They're going to put the word around and get back to me in a day or so. One of them seemed to know the name, not that he let on to me, of course. I kind of picked up on the way he paused before responding to me. I know Jed of old and how he reacts to things."

"Excellent news."

As if on cue, the first phone call came in. Donna answered the phone with her fingers crossed, only to hang up a few seconds later with a scowl on her face. "Some dickhead ringing up. He laughed and slammed the phone down."

"What is wrong with people? They can be such idiots. I hope a member of their family never has cause to need us in the future. They might realise how important it is to keep the phone lines clear during a murder enquiry."

"Wish we had the time to trace some of these calls. I'd love to see how they'd respond to having their arses hauled in and getting charged for wasting our time," Dave grumbled.

"If only life were that simple, Dave. I'll be in my office. Let me know if anything half-decent falls into our laps." Kayli stopped by the vending machine, collected a coffee then continued into the office. Closing the door, she took a sip from her cup and glanced out the window at the dreary sky overhead before rounding the desk to her chair. She picked up the phone and hesitated before she finally plucked up the courage to ring her brother. "Hi, Giles. It's only me. How are things? Or is that a dumb question?"

"Not dumb at all. I'm just about to leave for the hospital. Said I'd take Annabelle in a change of clothes."

"Oh, right. Is Bobby still with Mum and Dad?"

"Yes. As much as I wanted to bring him home here last night, I thought it would be too painful for me. Bizarre, I know."

"I think I would feel the same way in your situation, love. Your emotions must be all over the place."

M A Comley

"They are, but nothing compared to what Annabelle is feeling."

Kayli swallowed the lump that had forced its way into her throat. "I'm sorry, love. I'm wracked with guilt about what's happened."

Her brother remained silent for a few seconds.

She heard him sniff and figured he was overwhelmed and unable to speak. "Do you want me to go?"

"Yes, although I want to make sure you understand that neither Annabelle nor I blame you for what's occurred. Got that?"

"That's because you're wonderful people, kind and considerate until the last. No matter what you say, I'll still feel guilty about dragging you halfway around the world when Annabelle needed you."

"Nonsense. I'm not going to get in an argument about this, sis. Annabelle feels the same as I do. If it was meant to be, there was little we could do to prevent the child slipping away from us."

"Not sure I would be so sympathetic in your shoes. If you need me, just shout. However, I don't know why you'd do that when I had a devil of a job getting Bobby back to sleep last night."

"You're great with him. You just need to relax more when you're around him."

Kayli smiled. "Do you think he picks up on my anxiety? I'm so desperate to do the right thing by him, but it seems to prevent my brain from functioning properly when I'm around him."

"Kids are like dogs in that respect. They have a tendency to pick up when people are feeling insecure. You wait until you have kids of your own. You'll soon get to grips with how things work."

Kayli cringed. She didn't have the heart to insist that she had no intention of having kids, not in the near future at least. "I better go. I was just checking that everything was all right. Will you send my love and my apologies to Annabelle?"

"Nope. I'll send her your love but not your apology, because you're not at fault. If anything, I'm the one to blame for what's happened. If I hadn't jetted off with you like that, then maybe she'd still be carrying our child. I know I told you not to feel guilty about getting me involved. The truth is that the facts remain the same. I put Annabelle through nearly a week of unnecessary stress. That in itself couldn't have been good for the little one."

116

"Hey, listen to me. If you refuse to let me feel guilty, then the same goes for you, love. I found out something surprising from Mum last night."

"Oh, what's that?" he asked quietly.

"That she too suffered a miscarriage. She had it between giving birth to both of us. I was shocked by the revelation."

Giles gasped. "Really? I wonder why they both kept it a secret."

"Not sure. I suppose they had their reasons."

"Do you think that type of thing runs in the family? Like me having a miscarriage gene, if there is such a thing? Am I talking a load of bollocks here?"

"No, I don't think you're talking crap. Maybe it is hereditary and something worth delving into with your doctor before you plan on having any more kids."

"I'll have a quiet word with the doctor when I go in this evening. Not sure Annabelle will be up for having to deal with another pregnancy anytime soon anyway. This little one wasn't planned and sort of fell into our laps, if you get what I mean."

"I do. Mum told me that sometimes the body rejects a baby if it detects some degenerative abnormality in it."

"The doctor promised to go through the details with us later, felt the timing was wrong yesterday, not that we won't be grieving our loss for a long time to come."

"It's going to take a while to recover. We'll be here to support you both, though. Just shout if you need a hand with anything."

"Thanks, sis."

"Send our love to Annabelle and give her a gentle hug." Kayli hung up and sat back in her chair to contemplate their conversation. She had no doubt that the couple were strong enough to get through the ordeal. The question was how long they would have to endure such pain. Did a pain such as losing an infant ever dissipate?

She shook her head to clear her depressing thoughts and tackled her paperwork for the next half an hour or so until Dave knocked on her door around five. "Hi. Any news?"

"Graeme has come up trumps."

Kayli shot out of her chair. Wide-eyed, she asked, "As in located Nuttall?"

Dave smiled. "You've hit the nail on the head. I was wondering if you want to have the pleasure of picking the bastard up, or do you want me to send a patrol car to do the deed?"

Kayli slipped into her coat. "What do you think? Are you up for this?"

"Whoa, easy, tiger! Of course I'm up for it. I also think it would be far too dangerous for us to go over there alone."

"Are you talking armed response?" She reached into the top drawer of her desk and withdrew a Taser.

He laughed. "We can go it alone if that's what you want, as long as we're armed."

"'Armed and fully trained' is what you should have said, partner. Let's shake a leg and pick the bugger up."

They rushed down the stairs and through the reception area. There was a group of uniformed officers holding some kind of meeting with the desk sergeant as they passed through.

"Any of you guys want to tag along with us to pick up a possible murderer?"

The four uniformed officers all turned to face her. The desk sergeant's ears pricked up. "Watson and Clark, go with DI Bright. The rest of you, get on with what we've just discussed."

"Thanks, Sergeant. Follow us, men," she called over her shoulder after she'd barged through the large exit doors.

Dave had trouble keeping up with her. "Slow down. Maybe you should have brought Graeme instead."

"It's not too late. I can ring him if you want. I'm sure he'd jump at the chance to ride alongside me on a possible arrest."

"I was only joking. I'll be right in a second or two."

Kayli jumped in the car and started the engine. Dave joined her and swiftly sorted out his crutches as she revved the engine impatiently. Once Dave was comfortable, Kayli put her foot down, with the squad car close on her tail. They used their sirens until they got close to the address Graeme had given them.

"Shit, it's a slum. Graeme said he was hiding out in a squat," Dave said.

"God, I hate these places. They're usually full of drug users and prostitutes."

"I suppose their argument would be that society doesn't want or need them, so they can exist how they like."

"Yeah, but squatting in someone else's property is a bit too much, right?" Kayli said angrily.

"Don't have a go at me. I'm just looking at it from their point of view."

Kayli snorted. "Well, that's a first for you. Do you want to stay here?"

"Not likely. I'll let the guys accompany you into the house and stand guard on the door in case the weasel tries to make a run for it again."

"You can't cover both exits. I'll take one of the constables in with me and send the other one around the back to cover that exit," Kayli said, her eyes narrowed as she hatched her plan.

Dave nodded, and they both left the vehicle. After Kayli had filled in the two constables, they all moved into position before she rang the bell. A girl no older than eighteen opened the door, looking stoned out of her mind. She was wearing nothing more than a mid-thigh nightshirt.

"Yeah? What do you want?" She turned to shout over her shoulder, "Stand by your beds, guys. It's the filth."

Kayli forced her way past the bewildered girl.

It took a while for her to fathom that Kayli and the constable had entered the house uninvited. "Hey, you can't go barging in here like that. We've got rights."

Kayli tilted her head and lifted an eyebrow. "Seriously? Has someone brainwashed you with that idea, or did you think that up all by yourself?"

"Sarcastic cow," the girl mumbled. She slammed the front door shut and barged past Kayli and the constable.

"Aren't you going to ask why we're here?"

"Nope. I'm not fucking interested. You lot always cause bother when you show up here anyway. Why should this time be any different?"

Kayli shrugged. "I want to see Bob Nuttall."

"Don't know him. You sure you've got the right address?"

119

"I'm sure. He would have arrived here in the last few days. Does that help?"

The young woman scratched the side of her face. "Nope. Help yourselves. I ain't gonna do your work for you."

"Thanks for your assistance," Kayli growled.

"Whatever." They watched the girl go up the stairs, not concerned that her nightshirt was rising up to reveal the cheeks of her backside.

Kayli dug the constable in the ribs. "Avert your eyes, Constable, before you go blind."

His mouth opened and shut as he tried to think of an acceptable excuse for his lecherous behaviour.

Kayli chuckled when nothing was forthcoming. "Right, serious heads on now. I think we should stick together and search every room."

"Do you have a picture of the suspect, ma'am?"

Kayli dug out the mugshot she had stuffed in her jacket pocket before leaving the station and held it up for the constable. "Be careful. He's got a record as long as your arm."

The constable nodded and pointed at the first door on the right in the narrow hallway. "In here?"

"Seems as good a place as any to start."

The constable opened the door and switched on the light. Considering it was approaching five thirty, she was stunned to see that most of the inhabitants in the room were either under the bedclothes or lying on top of the makeshift beds spread out across the floor. "I'm looking for Bob Nuttall."

Kayli's request was met with silence. She nodded for the constable to circulate the room with her. They lifted sleeping bags and quilts to reveal the people hiding beneath them. Unfortunately, no one matched Nuttall's description.

Kayli heard the floorboards creaking overhead. She rushed to the door, and the constable joined her. "I'm hearing movement upstairs. I'm thinking we should go up there before he makes up his mind to shimmy down the drainpipe or something. He's already absconded from us once this week."

The constable nodded and ran ahead of her. At the top of the stairs, just coming out of one of the rooms, was the man himself. He took a swing at the constable and knocked him to the floor.

Kayli withdrew her Taser and pointed it at Nuttall. "Go on, give me a reason to use this."

"Get out of my way, bitch. You ain't got the guts to use that thing."

The constable struggled to his feet beside Nuttall.

"Stand back, Constable. Mr. Nuttall obviously wants to see what I'm made of." Without hesitation, she fired the Taser.

The barbs struck Nuttall in the chest. He cried out and collapsed to the floor immediately and was writhing around in pain until Kayli relinquished the pressure on the weapon's trigger. The constable, forgetting about his own injury, pounced on Nuttall, pulled his arms behind him and slapped the cuffs on his wrists before yanking the man to his feet. Nuttall tottered for a few seconds.

"Let him catch his breath before we escort him off the premises, Constable."

The constable nodded and placed Nuttall against the wall for a few moments.

"Right. Are you ready to cooperate with us, Mr. Nuttall?"

His head sank onto his chest. "I suppose so. Answer me this first—why are you being so heavy-handed with me?"

"How do you expect us to treat scum who murder innocent people?"

He shook his head as if to clear the fuzziness. "What the fuck are you talking about? I've never murdered anyone. You're crazy!" He tried to wrestle free of the constable latched on to his arm. "What proof do you have?"

"When we called at the flats the other day, you absconded the scene. That's as much proof as I need right now. Let's take him in, Constable."

Nuttall tried to twist out of the constable's grasp all the way through the house and continued his attempt until the constable placed him in the back seat of his vehicle.

"At last, thank God!" Dave said as soon as he saw they'd captured the culprit.

"Do you want to fetch your colleague? We'll watch him," Kayli suggested.

The constable ran up the side alley, and the two men returned moments later. "We'll follow you back to the station."

Kayli and Dave got back in their car. "Did he say anything?" Dave asked.

"Only the usual denial. I must admit that he looked pretty convincing when he denied the accusation."

"It has to be him. Don't start questioning yourself, not at this late stage."

"We need to see what Forensics come up with. If they can corroborate that he was there through DNA, then his denial will be useless."

"Are you going to question him tonight?"

Kayli turned to look at him. "You know that ain't going to happen. I prefer to let the weasels stew overnight in a cell."

"I know. But what about the time issue? You've got twenty-four hours to question him. You really think he's going to crack in that time?"

"Not sure. I need the forensics results to hand before I can question him hard, though. Let me think about it on the return journey."

"In other words, you want me to stay schtum so you can mull it over."

Kayli smiled. "In a nutshell, yes."

They arrived at the station around twenty minutes later. The desk sergeant booked Nuttall in and requested DNA samples from the man. Surprisingly, Nuttall agreed to the request without any form of resistance, again raising doubt in Kayli's mind. She knew how other prisoners usually reacted, and he was showing none of those signs. He had denied the charge from the outset and attempted to get out of his restraints, but he seemed relatively subdued as Kayli watched the sergeant go through the arrest form.

Dave was lingering impatiently a few feet away from her.

"Why don't you go and break the news to the rest of the team? I'll be up soon."

Her partner looked peeved at the prospect of climbing the stairs only to leave in another ten or fifteen minutes to go home.

The desk sergeant motioned for Kayli to join him. "Did you want me to set up an interview room for you, ma'am?"

Kayli lowered her voice so Nuttall couldn't hear. "Nope, he can suffer overnight. I'll question him first thing in the morning, Ray."

"Very well, ma'am. We'll feed and water him and tuck him up for the night."

"What you can do for me is arrange for the duty solicitor to be here at nine so we can proceed without delay. That is, unless Nuttall wants his own brief to attend. I'll leave that with you."

"I'll sort it all out for you, ma'am."

"Thanks, Ray."

Kayli's weary legs carried her up the stairs. The jubilation the team were feeling at capturing their man was obvious as soon as she entered the room. "Great job, team. Let's call it a day and start afresh in the morning. I've arranged for Nuttall to be questioned at nine. I'll be here around eight to check over the details of the case to ensure we haven't missed anything before I hit him with the evidence. Damn, I need to ring the pathologist in Wales, see if he's found any form of DNA on Potts's body."

"Do you want us all to come in early, boss?" Donna asked.

The others looked at her expectantly.

"You needn't. The choice is yours. Go home and get some rest, guys."

"We'll be here at eight or thereabouts," Dave called over his shoulder as he hobbled towards the door.

"You're fabulous, but you all know that, right?"

"We do." Graeme switched off his monitor and stood up to leave.

Kayli rushed into her office and dialled the pathologist. "Hello, this is DI Bright. Is that Mr. Hughes?"

"Ah, yes, Inspector. Please drop the formalities. It's Greg. What can I do for you?"

"I wanted to bring you up to date on where the investigation stands. We've arrested our main suspect. Obviously, that will mean we'll need you to tell us what DNA, if anything, was found at the scene."

"As yet, we haven't found anything, I'm afraid. Probably due to the amount of water the car was submerged in. What I do have for you is a brief outline of the post-mortem, if that will help."

"Excellent news. I've got a pen handy. Go ahead."

"I've really nothing new to add from what I told you at the scene. What I can confirm is that the back of his head had caved in a little from the force of the blow he received, and as I suspected, he drowned in the boot of his car."

"Do you think he was conscious throughout?"

"Highly unlikely, but I have no way of telling that. It was obviously a substantial blow in the first place that probably rendered him unconscious. He might have regained consciousness during the journey. The motion might have brought him round. Again, that's all speculation. For the family's sake, I'm inclined to say that it's unlikely that he regained consciousness."

"Okay, Greg, I'm willing to go along with that. His daughter is a little fragile at present, as you can imagine. Thanks for the update. I'll ensure the suspect's DNA profile is sent over to you tomorrow, in case you need it in the future."

"Excellent. Well done on capturing your man, Inspector."

"Thank you. I'll be in touch soon." Kayli ended the call, leaned back in her chair and let out a long, relieved sigh. It had been a hectic twenty-four hours, and the previous night's lack of sleep was beginning to catch up to her. She jumped out of her chair and shook out her arms and legs to reinvigorate herself before she started on her journey home.

She left the room, switched off all the lights and made her way out to the car. When she arrived home thirty minutes later, Mark was standing on the doorstep, waiting for her.

Kayli was frantic, fearing the worst, and rushed from the car. "What is it? Is it Annabelle? Has something happened to her?"

Mark drew her into his arms and kissed the top of her head. "Hey, everything is fine. Why are you so anxious?"

She slumped against his chest. Listening to his beating heart was an added calming influence. "One of those days. I'm tired, and my senses are in tatters, I suppose."

"Do you want to talk about it over dinner? I'll have to leave in an hour or so, though."

"Have you cooked again?"

He pushed her away from him. "Of course. It's nothing fancy. Fish, chips and peas, all from the freezer, if that's okay?"

"That's brilliant. Thanks for being so thoughtful. I'm starving."

Mark led the way into the house. In the lounge, she found a huge bouquet of flowers sitting on the coffee table with a small box of chocolates alongside it.

"Dare I ask? Are they for me?"

"No, they're for my bit on the side. Of course they're for you. I wanted to cheer you up and show you how much I love you."

Kayli's eyes misted up. They shared a long, lingering kiss. "You're amazing. Not sure what I've done to deserve being treated like a princess, but it is definitely appreciated. Is dinner ready?"

"You're my princess and worthy of being spoilt. Two minutes for dinner, so if you want to get changed, I'll dish up."

Kayli rushed upstairs and changed into her velour leisure suit, the one she always used to exercise in, not that she'd had much time to do that lately. She joined Mark in the kitchen, where they laughed and talked during their scrumptious meal.

"Why does food always taste better when someone else has cooked it?"

Mark laughed. "Can't say I've noticed that. It tasted all right to me."

"I think you're a better cook than me. Maybe that's the real answer."

"I wouldn't say that. I've had more time to prepare it during the day. Saying that, it was only a matter of opening up a few packets and shoving the items in the oven. Hardly *MasterChef* qualities needed for that. Glad you enjoyed it. Tough day at work?"

"Yes and no. We found the victim's body and had to go and break the news to the family, then we caught a break and discovered where the suspect was hiding out."

"Wow! Are you going to arrest the suspect tomorrow?" Mark asked, frowning.

"Nope, all done and dusted. He's in a police cell now. I'll question him in the morning. I'll prepare my questions this evening while you're at work."

Mark placed a hand over hers. "You're amazing. Can't the questions wait? You could do with a rest this evening after what went on last night."

She smiled at him. "I guess, but the team have agreed to start at eight in the morning. I could brainstorm with them for an hour before I hit the interview room with the suspect."

"That's my girl. Shame I can't pull a sickie and join you. Not sure the boss would take kindly to me doing that at this early stage in my career."

Kayli chuckled. "I'll probably fall asleep not long after you leave anyway."

They cleared up the kitchen together, and while Kayli made a coffee, Mark went upstairs to get changed. He reappeared a few minutes later, dressed in his suit.

"I'll miss you this evening," she said, sashaying towards him.

He held her at arm's length. "Don't. I feel bad enough leaving you every night as it is."

"Let's hope something else comes your way soon."

"The money is good, so it'll do for now."

They drank their coffees wrapped in each other's arms, then it was time for Mark to leave. The house seemed empty the second he walked out the front door. Kayli waved at him from the lounge window then switched on the TV. She flicked through an interior-design magazine for the next fifteen minutes before her eyelids began to droop. Even though it was only seven forty-five, she locked up the house and went to bed, exhausted.

CHAPTER TEN

Kayli stretched out a hand and slid it over Mark's back. She had been so exhausted that she hadn't stirred when he slipped in beside her. Despite all her misgivings about not being able to sleep properly when he wasn't there, she'd had no trouble. Last night had been exceptional, however. So the jury was still out for her as far as his job was concerned.

Deciding not to disturb Mark, she eased out of bed and into the bathroom for a shower. Then she crept back into the bedroom, collected the clothes she had laid out to wear the night before and went into the spare room to get dressed. Kayli poked her head round the door to see if Mark had stirred at all. He hadn't, so she left him to sleep, quietly descended the stairs and left the house without having anything to eat. She had already made the decision to call in at the baker's on the way to work. After choosing a selection of cakes and picking out a few croissants, she continued her journey into work.

The team were already there when she arrived.

"Dave, can you buy the coffees? I stopped off for breakfast, so I hope you guys haven't eaten. I think I bought enough for the whole station to share." She chuckled.

Over breakfast, the team raised certain points that they felt Kayli should ask the suspect during the interview. Kayli jotted down a few notes of her own, wiped her mouth on a serviette, topped up her lipstick and announced to Dave that she was ready. "Ready?"

He jumped to his feet. "As I'll ever be. I wouldn't miss this for the world."

They made their way down the stairs, where the desk sergeant motioned for Kayli to join him in reception.

"Everything all right, Ray?"

"Yes, ma'am. The duty solicitor is here already. I'm just about to send a constable to collect the suspect. Room Two is ready for you."

"Excellent news." Kayli wandered over to the young woman sitting in the reception area with a briefcase leaning up against her slim ankle. Extending her hand, she introduced herself. "DI Kayli Bright. I don't think I've had the pleasure of meeting you before, Miss..."

"Belinda Cooper. It's a pleasure to meet you, Inspector. I've heard a lot of good things about you."

Kayli raised an eyebrow. "That's good to know. I'm a fair copper, Belinda, as you'll soon discover. What I won't take is bullshit from a suspect, however. Keep your client in line and working with us, and everything should be fine. If he starts slinging around the 'no comments', I'm afraid you'll see an entirely different side of me."

She smiled. "Understood. I'm inclined to agree with you. I never advise my clients going down the 'no comment' route. It serves no purpose and wastes everyone's time. Leave him to me. Can I have a quick word with him before we begin?"

"I can arrange that. Give me two minutes." Kayli walked back to the sergeant's desk. "She wants a brief chat with Nuttall. I'd let her visit him in his cell for a few minutes. Leave the door open and a constable on guard at the door. That should do."

"I'll arrange it now, ma'am." He turned to instruct one of the constables rifling through paperwork alongside him. The constable collected the solicitor and showed her down the hallway into Nuttall's cell.

"Come on, Dave. We'll go to the interview room and get the equipment set up while we wait for them to reappear."

They had only been in the room for a few minutes before the door opened. The suspect, accompanied by his solicitor and the constable, walked into the room.

"Take a seat, Mr. Nuttall. We have a few formalities to attend to first before we can begin."

"The sooner we get on with this, the better in my book. You ain't got anything on me. This should be a breeze for her to handle," he said, nodding towards his solicitor.

"We'll see." Kayli gave the man the tightest smile she could muster.

Dave said the necessary verbiage for the disc, announcing the time, date and who was present in the room.

Kayli glanced at her notes. "Okay, I'm going to call you Bob, if that's all right with you?"

Nuttall shrugged. "Whatever, just get on with it. Before you start, I want to say again that I haven't done anything wrong. This is all a big mistake, as you'll find, to your cost. I've had a word with my solicitor, and I'll be suing you for false arrest and holding me in a police cell overnight."

"Thank you for the warning, sir. Maybe you can tell me why you absconded from your flat when we knocked on your door on Monday."

"I didn't."

"I think that's a lie and doesn't bode well going forward, if indeed you're intent on proving your innocence."

He slumped back in his chair and crossed his arms defiantly. "All right, I did run."

"Why?" she asked, a moment of triumph flowing through her veins.

"The truth is I don't know."

Kayli raised her eyebrows. "You expect us to believe that? Do you make a habit of running off every time there is a knock on your door, Bob? After all, you had no idea we were the police. Surely only a person who has something to hide would abscond like that. True?"

"I saw you arrive and figured you were the police."

Kayli cast her mind back to the layout of the flats and knew he was lying. "If I remember rightly, your flat is at the top of the house. There is a fire escape—the exit you took—to the rear of the property and no other windows in your flat. There is no way you could have seen us arrive at the property as we pulled up at the front and used that entrance to gain access to the property."

His head dipped onto his chest, and he remained silent.

Kayli's gaze met Belinda's. The solicitor leaned over and whispered something in her client's ear.

"Shall we try that again?" Kayli asked. "Why did you run, Bob?"

"I panicked," he admitted with a certain degree of reluctance edging his tone.

"Panicked why?"

"Because I thought it was the landlord and he was about to turf me out."

Kayli glanced at her partner, who looked up from taking notes. She turned back to look at Nuttall. "Am I right in saying that you had an argument with your landlord on the Saturday of the previous week?"

"Yes."

"May I ask what that argument was about?"

He sighed. "I didn't have the funds to pay the rent." His gaze drifted down to the table once more.

Kayli tapped her fingers on the table. "Come now, Bob. We both know that's a lie, don't we?"

His gaze met hers and narrowed. "Not sure what you're getting at."

Kayli smiled and tilted her head. She pushed a photo of the money they had found under his floorboards across the desk to him. "We didn't have time to count it, but a rough guesstimate would put it at around a hundred grand. How did I do?"

He shook his head. "The money ain't mine, I tell you. I'm holding it for someone."

"You are? Why? And what's their name so that we can verify your claim?"

He shuffled his feet a while before he answered. "I mean it. It's not mine, but I can't give you a name. That's all I can tell you about the money. It has nothing to do with Potts, though."

"I fail to see how. You had nearly a hundred grand buried beneath the floorboards in your landlord's house, and yet you refused to pay him the rent that was due, and you're telling me that didn't concern him."

"Because it was someone else's money, I tell you. If it had been mine, I would have paid him what was due."

Kayli ran a hand over her face as she thought. "Okay, you want to know what I think?"

"Surprise me," he snarled.

"I have a different scenario running through my mind, one that involves a large sum of money in exchange for you carrying out a favour. Want to know what that favour is, Bob?"

His eyes narrowed further.

"Maybe someone paid you a significant sum of money to kill Paul Potts and dispose of his body. How am I doing here?"

Nuttall shook his head and sat forward to perch on the edge of his seat. "That's utter bollocks, and you can't prove a damn thing. Why the fuck would I accept a deal like that? I'm not a bloody murderer. What would be my motive?"

"Ex-cons notoriously struggle in the outside world when they come out. You saw the opportunity and grasped it with both hands to make some real cash."

He continually shook his head as his cheeks grew redder with every word she said. "Utter bullshit. What do you take me for? I ain't killed no one in my life before. Have you even checked my record to see what I was banged up for?"

"We have. Stealing cars. But that doesn't prove a thing. Prisoners talk amongst themselves, hatch plans all the time, seeking opportunities in which to possibly line their pockets more. Is that how it went down, Bob? You got greedy and bumped your landlord off and disposed of his body?"

He banged his clenched fist on the desk, making everyone in the room jump. "That's fucking crap! I'm telling you the truth. I had no idea that Potts was even dead. I liked the man… well, maybe 'liked' is a bit over the top. I had no problems with him."

"And yet you were heard arguing with Paul Potts on Saturday. Are you denying that?"

"No. I admit we had a falling out. I just didn't have rent money. That doesn't mean I killed the fecker! Jesus, okay, if it's going to clear my name, you want to know what the money is all about?"

"Enlighten me," Kayli replied sarcastically.

"Cars. I've stolen two cars to order recently, and that's the payoff I got. The only thing is I have to pay a majority of that money to Roger Stills on the inside when he comes out. He put me in touch with a bunch of people. You can check with him. He'll probably say I'm telling a pack of lies, but I swear it's the truth."

Something in the man's eyes told Kayli that he was being honest. "We'll check out your story and get back to you. Until then, you'll remain in custody."

"You can't do that. I've done nothing wrong."

Kayli laughed then said to Belinda, "You might want to have a word with your client. He's under the misapprehension that stealing cars to order is a legitimate business."

"I'll do that, Inspector. Are we finished here?"

"We are." Kayli gestured for Dave to end the interview and motioned for the constable to return Nuttall to his cell. "We'll be in touch soon, Mr. Nuttall, once we've corroborated your story."

"What? Can they keep me here like this?" he asked his solicitor, mortified.

"I'm afraid they can, within reason. I'm sure the inspector will make contact with Mr. Stills at the earliest opportunity and get things cleared up quickly."

"I will. You have my word on that."

The constable tapped Nuttall on his shoulder then escorted him from the room.

Kayli walked the solicitor to the reception area and shook her hand. "I'll be in touch as soon as I hear anything. What's your take on his story?"

Belinda hitched up her right shoulder. "He seemed pretty genuine to me, but who knows nowadays?"

"Exactly. I can't take the risk of taking what he says at face value. Thanks for coming in."

She watched the solicitor leave the station then followed Dave up the stairs. "What did you think of all that?"

"I hate to say this, but he seemed pretty convincing to me, and his story had a ring of truth to it. It'll be interesting to see when this Roger Stills is due to be released."

"I'm going to get Donna on it right away. One step forward and two steps back. So bloody annoying."

"Yep. If it turns out he's telling the truth, then what are we left with?"

Kayli nodded. "Absolutely bugger all—that's what."

CHAPTER ELEVEN

Donna got to work straight away and delivered the results within half an hour. She knocked on Kayli's office door and walked into the room.

"Take a seat, Donna. What have you discovered?"

"Roger Stills is in Parkhurst Prison. He was indeed Bob Nuttall's cellmate for a few months before his release."

"Damn! Parkhurst? I don't have the time to visit the Isle of Wight just to ask a few questions."

"Can we get either the local force or the governor to question him for us?"

"We can certainly try. Can you get me the number of the prison?"

The ever-efficient constable smiled and slid a piece of paper across the table. "Governor Smythe's number. He's expecting your call," Donna said with a glint in her eye.

"You're a star. Thanks, Donna."

After Donna left the office, Kayli placed the call to the governor. "Hello, Governor Smythe. This is DI Kayli Bright of the Avon and Somerset Constabulary. Thank you for accepting my call."

"You're welcome, Inspector. I'm happy to help if I can."

Kayli gave him a brief rundown of the nature of her call. "You can see why it's so urgent that we find out if Nuttall is telling us the truth or not."

"I can. Do you want to leave it with me? I promise to get back to you this afternoon once I've questioned Stills."

"That would be wonderful. What's the likelihood of him opening up to you?"

"Well, he's due to be released in a few weeks, if he behaves himself, if you get my drift."

Kayli chuckled. "I do. Thanks for your cooperation on this matter, Governor Smythe."

"No problem. I'll ring you sometime after lunch."

Kayli ended the call and stared out the window, reflecting on which direction the investigation should go next. The media appeal had led them to Nuttall, but that link had become tenuous at best. She sighed and began to tackle the pile of paperwork sitting on her desk.

Donna fetched her in a coffee around an hour later. "Any luck, boss?"

"Sorry, I should have updated you all. The governor is going to question Stills and get back to me this afternoon. How are things going out there?"

"Umm… I think Graeme has something he'd like to share with you, if you have the time."

"Always have the time if it's to do with an ongoing investigation, Donna." She rose from her seat and walked out of the office, towards Graeme's desk. "Donna says you might have something for us to go on, Graeme. I have my fingers crossed, because we haven't got much as it is."

"I know how frustrated we all are with regard to Nuttall, so I thought I'd look back on the ANPR footage, and I discovered this." He pointed at a couple of vehicles on the screen.

Confused, Kayli asked, "What am I supposed to be looking at?"

"When I was trying to find Paul Potts's car, I was focused on which route it took, but on second viewing, I noticed that he, or whoever was driving his car, was being followed."

"You're saying there's a second car?"

"Yes, not directly behind Potts's car, but here." He pointed at the screen again, specifically indicating a small blue Fiat.

"This is excellent news and could be the getaway car the murderer made his escape in. It also indicates that two people were in on the murder if Paul was already in the boot at that time."

Graeme smiled and nodded. "My sentiments exactly."

"Tell me you've managed to locate the registration number on that vehicle."

Graeme tutted and shook his head. "Sorry, no. It was travelling too close to the car in front and the angle on the back wasn't good either."

"As if they knew we'd be on the lookout for them—is that what you're saying?"

"That's my take on it."

Kayli sighed and chewed her lip. "What about the driver? Can you enhance the picture to get a close-up of the driver, perhaps?"

"I've tried, and it's impossible."

"Have you got anything at all? Are we looking at a male or female driver?"

"Again, it's difficult, near impossible, to tell. The pictures are hazy and only take in the upper torso and not the head or face. Frustrating, I know. All I can do is keep trawling over the footage and see if I can catch a break somewhere along the line."

"I'll leave it with you. Damn, that's my phone ringing." Kayli ran into her office and picked up the phone before it rang off. "Hello. DI Bright. How can I help?"

"Ah… you're there. Sorry, this is Samuel Potts, Inspector." The man sounded distant and confused.

"Hello there, Mr. Potts. Is everything okay?"

"Not really. I didn't know who to ring. Of course, I rang for an ambulance right away, then my mind went blank until I put my hand in my pocket and found your card."

The man was rambling, and Kayli was concerned when he mentioned he'd called an ambulance. "Nice and slowly, Samuel. Why have you called an ambulance?"

"It's Anita. I found her at the house, barely breathing."

"What? Is she okay? Did she try to take her own life?"

"It looks that way." His voice caught in his throat. "They're dealing with her now."

"At the house? Is that where you are?"

"No. We're at the hospital. I didn't know who to turn to. I can't lose her, as well. Please God, don't let this happen."

"Okay, stay calm. Are you at A&E?"

"Yes. Please tell me what I should do, Inspector."

"Stay where you are. I'm on my way."

"Thank you. I'll see you soon."

Kayli slammed the phone back into its docking station, grabbed her handbag and rushed into the incident room. "Damn, looks like

Anita Potts has tried to end her life. I'm going to A&E. No need for you to come, Dave. Will you man my phone in case Governor Smythe rings back?"

"Sure. Leave everything to me and just go. Hope she's okay when you get there," Dave replied, looking shocked.

"So do I."

Kayli used her siren to get to the hospital. She tore through the doors to the entrance of the Accident and Emergency Department at Bristol Royal Infirmary, flashed her ID at the young redhead on reception and asked where she could find Anita Potts.

"They're treating her now. Her uncle is waiting in the family room."

"Which is where?"

"First door on the right."

"Thank you." She trotted along the hallway and into the room, where she found a distraught Samuel, his head bowed, staring at the floor. He looked up as she entered the room, and a brief smile touched his lips.

Kayli sat down in the chair next to him. "Hello, Samuel. Any news on how Anita is?"

"Not yet. They've just left me here to think all sorts. What if I lose her? I'll never forgive myself for not taking care of her in her hour of need. Paul would be looking down on me in shame."

Kayli gathered his shaking hands in her own. "That's nonsense. No one could have predicted she would be driven to do something like this. You can't blame yourself. I won't allow you to," she added, smiling.

"That's kind of you to say so, Inspector, but the guilt still remains. I should have done more."

"Let me go and find a doctor, see what's going on. I'll be right back."

She heard him mutter a *thank you* before she left the room. She made her way down the corridor to the cubicles and lingered there for several minutes before a doctor appeared.

"Hello, Doctor." She held up her warrant card as he came out of one of the cubicles. "I'm sorry to trouble you. I wanted to know what was happening with Anita Potts. Suspected attempted suicide."

He smiled tautly. "One moment please." The doctor slipped through the swinging doors at the end of the corridor and emerged a few minutes later. "She's okay. They're about to pump her stomach, then they'll transfer her up to the women's ward. The doctor dealing with her will come and apprise you of the situation soon. Can you wait in the family room until then?"

"Of course. I appreciate your help. Sorry to inconvenience you."

"Not at all."

Kayli turned and made her way back to the family room. Samuel looked up at her as soon as she entered. Kayli raised a hand in front of her. "She's fine. They're going to pump her stomach then move her to a ward. We should be able to see her soon."

He buried his head in his hands and sobbed.

Kayli sat down beside him and ran a hand over his back to comfort him. "She'll get through this. We'll get her the help she needs to aid her recovery. Don't worry, Samuel."

He withdrew a cotton handkerchief from his pocket and blew his nose. "Thank you. I'm not sure I would have coped if I'd lost her, not so soon after losing Paul."

They sat there in silence for a few more minutes, until a young Asian doctor walked into the room. "Anita Potts's family?"

"This is her uncle Samuel, and I'm DI Kayli Bright. I'm working with the family regarding another matter. What news do you have for us, Doctor?"

"Pleased to meet you. Well, let me say that your niece is a very lucky girl that you arrived at the house when you did. Another five minutes, and I would have been signing her death certificate."

"Really? She's very fortunate, then. Is she awake, Doctor? Can we see her?"

"She came to for a little bit. We've pumped her stomach to rid it of its damaging contents, then I gave her a sedative to knock her out for a little while to allow her body to recover without her feeling anxious about anything."

"Okay. Did she take pills, Doctor?"

"Yes, Zopiclone. Were you aware that she was taking sleeping medication, Mr. Potts?"

Samuel's brow furrowed. "No, I had no idea."

The doctor plucked a small tub from his pocket and studied it.

Kayli noticed him frowning. "What's wrong, Doctor?"

"It's the name. I hadn't noticed it before." He showed the pot to Kayli.

Kayli studied the pot then asked, "Mabel Wilson. Samuel, do you know of anyone by that name?"

He shook his head. "Not off the top of my head."

"Anita has never mentioned a friend with that name whom she visits?" Kayli prompted.

He ran a hand through his grey hair as he thought. "No. But then my mind is all over the place, Inspector."

"Never mind. Can I take this, Doctor?"

"Of course. The pot was empty when the paramedic handed it to me. He told me it was lying on the floor next to Anita."

"One last question before I let you get on, Doctor. Did Anita say why she did it? Or did she speak at all?"

"She whispered something. I bent down to hear what she was saying, and it sounded like *Sharon*."

"That makes sense. Sharon is her stepsister. I'll get in touch with her, tell her that Anita is here. Thank you for caring for her."

"That's what we're here for. She will need to have a psych evaluation before she's discharged. It's nothing to worry about. She can talk over any anxieties she has at present."

"Her father was murdered a few days ago. I had to break the news to Samuel and Anita that I had discovered his body only yesterday."

"Ah… I see. I suppose her actions are understandable, given the circumstances." The doctor shook their hands and left the room.

"Are you all right, Samuel?" Kayli asked, rubbing his upper arm.

"I'm still coming to terms with things. Why would a twenty-four-year-old young woman choose to end her own life?"

"I'll never understand the emotional turmoil and angst people must be feeling to do such a thing. Most people think it's the coward's way out, but I don't believe that. It takes a lot of guts to even contemplate doing something so dreadful."

"I suppose. I never realised Anita had such feelings. When her mother died last year, she was the one who held that family together."

"Maybe she was still suffering the loss of her mother, and losing her father in such a vile manner was probably the element that tipped her over the edge."

"I suppose. I never thought to ring either Sharon or Dylan. I should have."

"Any reason why you didn't?"

"Not really, except that we're not all that close, not like Anita and I are. Do you want me to ring them?"

"I'll do it. No problem. You take a seat and rest for a little while. I'm sure the staff will come and fetch us soon once Anita has been transferred."

He sank into the chair again, and Kayli rang the station. "Donna, can you find me Sharon Potts's home phone number please?"

After a short delay, Donna relayed the number, and Kayli jotted it down in her notebook.

She ended the call and dialled the number. The answerphone picked it up. Kayli refused to leave such a personal message on the machine. Once Anita was settled on the ward and she was happy to leave her and Samuel, Kayli would drop by the care home where Sharon worked and break the news to her.

~ ~ ~

Twenty-five minutes later, a nurse took Samuel and Kayli upstairs to the women's ward. Samuel insisted that Kayli leave the hospital and try to find Sharon.

After receiving Samuel's blessing, Kayli jumped in the car and drove to the Nightingale Care Home. It was a crescent-shaped red-brick building consisting of four floors. The gardens at the front had colourful shrubs still in bloom despite the time of year.

Kayli walked through the main doors and approached an elderly woman wearing spectacles sitting behind the reception desk.

"Hello there. Can I help you?"

"I was hoping to speak to Sharon Potts, who works here."

The woman gasped. "The staff aren't supposed to have personal visits during working hours."

"I'm sorry. I would regard this as an emergency. I'm DI Kayli Bright. Maybe I should speak to the manager."

"Oh, okay. Well, that throws a different light on things. Let me get Mrs. Addison for you."

Kayli walked away from the desk and over towards the notice-board. Out of the corner of her eye, she saw a figure, one that she felt was watching her. She turned swiftly, but the person had gone. *That's strange!*

"Hello, I'm Sylvia Addison. You wanted to see me, Inspector?"

"Gosh, you scared the life out of me. Sorry, yes. I asked to see Sharon Potts, but the receptionist wouldn't allow me to speak to her during working hours. I wouldn't normally go over someone's head like this, but I have news of a family emergency that Sharon needs to be made aware of. Is it possible for me to see her?"

"Oh dear, I'm sorry to hear that. I'm sure we can make an exception to the rule in this instance. Let me try and locate her for you. Marjorie, can you have a wander around for me, see if you can find Sharon? I'll watch the desk in your absence."

The disgruntled woman left her seat and marched up the hallway, disappearing around the corner at the top.

"Sorry to cause this much trouble," Kayli said, glancing out the front door at the garden beyond.

"Honestly, it's fine. I hope you won't think I'm being nosy if I ask what the emergency is, Inspector."

"Can I ask how well you know Sharon?"

Mrs. Addison's brow creased. "She's worked here for about two years, so pretty well."

"Are you aware that she has a sister?"

"Of course. Has something happened to Anita?"

"I've just come from the hospital. Anita tried to take her own life this morning."

Mrs. Addison gasped. "Oh no, that's dreadful."

"Yes, and on top of what has happened to her father, the family aren't having much luck at present."

"You've lost me. Their father?"

It was Kayli's turn to frown. "He was reported missing the other day. I'm the SIO on the case. I had to inform Anita Potts and her uncle Samuel that we had discovered Paul Potts's body. We believe that's why Anita tried to end her life."

"Goodness me! That's terrible. How that family has suffered. Poor Sharon, carrying such a burden and continuing to work as if everything at home is just fine."

"I suppose people deal with grief differently. Some openly weep, while others choose to shove it aside and get on with their daily lives."

Kayli paced the area for the next ten minutes until a breathless Marjorie finally returned.

"Well? Where's Sharon?" Mrs. Addison asked.

Marjorie held her arms out to the sides. "I've hunted high and low for that girl and can't find her anywhere."

"Stay here. I'll go and look for her," Mrs. Addison stated sharply, looking anything but happy with the receptionist.

"Do you want me to come with you?" Kayli offered.

"You might as well. I'm sorry about this."

Kayli had trouble keeping up with the taller woman's long strides. She poked her head quickly into every room they came to.

"Nothing. Where on earth could she have gone? I thought she was assigned to the ground-floor patients this week, but maybe I'm wrong about that. Let's try upstairs."

They took the stairs up to the second level and repeated the process of searching every room, until something caught Kayli's eye. "Wait!" She pulled on Mrs. Addison's arm, halting her mid-stride.

"What is it?"

"Mrs. Wilson. What's her first name?"

"Mabel, I believe."

"Can you check, just to make sure for me? I'll explain why in a second."

"Let me check." Mrs. Addison poked her head back into the room she'd just left and asked the old lady sitting in the chair, "How are you doing today, Mabel?"

"I'm fine, dear. Always fine. Your staff always look after me so well."

"Enjoy the rest of your day, Mabel." Mrs. Addison stepped back into the hallway. "It's definitely Mabel. May I ask why?"

Kayli withdrew the small pot from her jacket pocket and gave it to the woman to examine. "Oh my! Where the dickens did you get this?"

Kayli ran a concerned hand over her face. "It was found beside Anita at her house."

"Are you saying she took these tablets to end her life?"

"Slight correction—attempt to end her life."

"What does this mean? That Sharon stole these tablets and gave them to her sister to take to help her sleep?"

"That's something along the lines of what I was thinking. Would you mind asking Mabel if she's noticed any of her tablets missing lately?"

"Without hesitation." Mrs. Addison opened the door for the third time in as many minutes. "It's only me again. Mabel, can you tell me if you've misplaced any of your medication lately?"

"Yes. I did. But Sharon said that I wasn't to worry, that she would pick up a repeat prescription for me."

"Has she done that for you yet?"

"Yes, she brought me my new pills yesterday. I only had one sleepless night, thank goodness. Such a lovely girl, so helpful and such a sweet, kind soul she has."

"As long as you've got a replacement prescription. Thank you."

"Not at all, dear. Thank you for employing such attentive staff."

Mrs. Addison closed the door, and her eyes widened in anger. "I want to know what's going on here, Inspector. The quicker we find Sharon Potts, the better, I think. Don't you?"

"I agree."

They continued their search with gusto this time. Unfortunately, they came to the same conclusion that Marjorie had earlier—Sharon was no longer on the premises.

"Do you have a clocking in system for the staff?" Kayli asked.

"Not really. They sign a register every time they either arrive or leave the building. In case we have a fire, you see. It's the law."

"Can you show me that register?"

"It's at the reception desk."

Together, they rushed back to the desk. Mrs. Addison flicked through the current pages in the register and pointed to Sharon's name. "There, she started her shift at midday. There is no reason for her to go missing."

"Do you happen to know what car she drives?" Kayli asked, her heart pounding.

"I don't. Marjorie, do you know?"

"I think it's a small car. Like a Fiat. I could be wrong, though."

Kayli ran towards the doors. "Thank you, ladies. You've been very helpful."

"Wait… where are you—" The door swung closed behind Kayli, cutting off what the manager was calling out after her.

Kayli drove back to the station faster than an express train could have carried her. She ran up the stairs to the station two at a time, her short legs not quite managing three steps in her haste. She barged through the door and into the incident room. Her three team members all looked startled by her entrance.

"Bloody hell, where's the damn fire?" Dave shouted.

"Donna, get me a glass of water while I catch my breath, will you?"

Donna shot out of her chair and delivered the glass of water within seconds. "Are you all right?" she asked.

"I will be in a minute." Kayli gulped down the cool liquid and placed a hand over her rapidly beating heart. "I think I know who the killer is."

"What? Who?" Dave asked, swivelling in his seat to face her.

"God, I hope I'm wrong, and I bloody well could be."

"Who?" Dave demanded, more urgently this time.

"The stepsister, Sharon Potts."

"No way!" Dave said, his face twisted in confusion.

She produced the pill pot and slammed it on the desk. "Yes way! The paramedics who attended the callout found this container sitting alongside Anita."

"And? Lots of people take pills to end it. What are you getting at?" Dave replied when Kayli paused to take a breath.

"The name printed on there is Mabel Wilson."

The three team members all sat forward in their seats, their interest piqued.

"The doctor told me that when Anita woke up, she was disorientated and only managed to say one word: Sharon. Originally,

I thought she was concerned about Sharon, so I said I would shoot over to where she works and inform her that Anita is in hospital and that she'd attempted to take her own life. When I arrived, Sharon was nowhere to be found. While I was standing in the reception area, I thought I saw someone watching me, but when I turned to look, that person had vanished." She took a large gulp of water then continued, "Anyway, the manager of the home searched for Sharon, and I volunteered to tag along. I spotted a patient named Mabel Wilson. The old lady confirmed that some of her tablets had gone missing in the last few days."

"Whoa! So you think Sharon took them and gave them to Anita?" Dave said, sitting back in his chair and interlocking his fingers on top of his head.

Donna narrowed her eyes. "Gave them to Anita or forced her to take them?"

Kayli pointed a finger at Donna. "Glad to see someone is keeping up with my way of thinking. We all know that Anita was in a vulnerable state. What if Sharon forced her to take the pills against her will, and that's what Anita was trying to tell the doctor when she mentioned Sharon's name?"

"That's a pretty big what-if," Dave replied.

"I know. Believe me, had Sharon been at her place of work, I doubt I would have gone down this line. The fact is I felt someone watching me, and when we searched the premises for Sharon, she was no longer at work. Too much of a coincidence for me." Kayli took another sip of water. "And that's not all. This is the most condemning lead yet. When I asked the manager what type of car Sharon drives, the receptionist told me it's—"

"A blue Fiat," Graeme finished for her.

"Correct. Now do you see why I'm so damned excited, Dave?"

He nodded. "Yep. I should have known you wouldn't go jumping the gun without something more substantial to back up your claims. What now?"

"We need to track her down. I doubt she'll go back home."

"What about her brother? Do you think he had anything to do with it? You know, the pills, or even the bigger picture, possibly involved with the father's death?"

"I think we have to err on the side of caution here. They share a house together, and they appear pretty close. My thinking is that he had to know what was going on. Don't forget, someone drove Paul Potts's car to that destination. If Sharon was following the vehicle in her car, then it seems a given that Dylan should be involved too. Again, at this point, it's all speculation. Graeme, I really need you to look at the ANPR and CCTV footage from a different angle now if at all possible. We need to place both the brother and the sister at the scene." Kayli stood up and walked towards Donna's desk. "Can you put in a request for a search warrant for Sharon and Dylan's house, Donna? It'll be good to have that in place for when we need to get in there."

"What about the brother? Do you want to pay him a visit?" Dave suggested.

"I'm thinking along those lines, Dave. I need to set up a surveillance team outside their house in case Sharon returns. We need an outside team for that as we have too much work to do between us around here. I'll have a word with the desk sergeant, see what he can come up with on that front."

"How is the kid doing now?" Dave asked. "Anita, I mean."

"The doctor gave her a sedative, and she was moved to the women's ward. Samuel has promised to ring me when she wakes up."

"What if Sharon turns up at the hospital to finish off the job?"

Kayli nodded. "I'll arrange for someone to guard Anita's room just in case. Donna, once you've sorted out the warrant, can you look up what car the brother drives for me? Then I think we should put out an alert on both vehicles. Actually, hold fire on the brother's car until Dave and I report back. Give me five minutes to have a word with the desk sergeant, Dave, then we'll pay the brother a discreet visit."

Kayli finished her glass of water and left the incident room. Her head was thumping along with her heart.

The desk sergeant's smile dissipated when he saw Kayli's serious expression. "Everything all right, ma'am?"

"I could do with some assistance if you have a couple of spare bodies, Ray."

"You only need to ask, ma'am. You know that. What do you need?"

"I need a couple of plain-clothes officers in a discreet car to carry out surveillance on an address. Do you have anyone who fits the bill?"

"I do. Jot down the address for me, and I'll get that sorted ASAP. Do you need anything else from me?"

Kayli smiled. "Yes, I have a witness in hospital I need to keep safe. Anita Potts. Would it be possible for you to send an officer to guard her room for me? No one in or out of the room except her uncle, the nursing team or me."

"I can't believe what I'm hearing. Of course. Consider it done."

"You're an absolute legend. That's the trouble with running a small team at times. My lot all have tasks they need to do in my absence."

"No problem. I completely understand. Is this to do with Paul Potts's murder? Are you saying that you think the person we have in custody is innocent?"

"Yes, that's the way the enquiry is going, Ray. Hopefully, we'll have a definitive answer by the end of the day."

"Samuel will be relieved."

Kayli smiled and patted him on the arm.

Dave hobbled into the reception area.

"Are you ready for the off, partner?" Kayli asked.

"Ready. Not sure if the body is able, but it's the only one I've got."

CHAPTER TWELVE

When they arrived at the pub, the place was experiencing the afternoon lull between the lunchtime and evening sittings. Kayli walked up to a man in his fifties, who stood erect with his shoulders back. The stance made his rotund belly protrude more than it would have otherwise.

She flashed her ID in the man's face. "DI Kayli Bright, and this is my partner, DS Dave Chaplin. Are you the manager of this establishment, sir?"

His brow wrinkled a little. "I am. Why would the police be knocking at my door, so to speak?"

"We'd like a chat with a member of your staff if he's available."

"Who might that be?"

"Dylan Potts. Is he on the premises, sir?"

"To be honest with you, I'm not sure. He was here serving at the lunchtime session, and he's due to work a shift this evening. I tend to let my staff have some time off during shifts. May I ask what this is about?"

"We're investigating a crime and wish to speak to him in connection with it. Do you know where he goes on his time off?"

"Home, I believe. You could try there. If he's not there, then I really have no clue. I don't keep tabs on what my staff get up to during their downtime, Inspector."

"Thank you, sir. You've been most helpful." Kayli and Dave began to walk towards the exit.

"What's the investigation? You never did say," the manager called after them.

Ignoring the man, Kayli continued out to the car. She slammed her clenched fist on the roof. "Damn. We need to go to the house."

"I have a suggestion to make if you're willing to listen." Dave smiled impishly.

"Don't look like that. When don't I listen to your suggestions?"

He rolled his eyes. "All right, no need to get antsy on me. I was only trying to lighten the mood."

Kayli tutted. "You can be such a pain in the rear at times. Get on with it, Dave."

"Donna's looking into what car Dylan drives, right?"

"Yes. What are you thinking?"

"Ring Donna, see if she's got the information yet, then we drive past the house to see if the car is there first before we reassess the situation and what we should do next. If it turns out that Sharon and Dylan are both involved in their stepfather's death, then we need to be cautious. The last thing we want is to go marching in there unarmed."

"I think you're right. Let's go. If his car is there, then we'll place a call for backup and get armed officers to join us."

They both jumped in the car and set off. Kayli's heart was pounding so much that she could feel it pulsing at the pressure points all over her body. "We need to figure out why Sharon and Dylan would kill their stepfather. We haven't touched on a possible motive yet."

"Maybe he abused them as kids, and they waited this long to exact their revenge."

"Maybe. I can't discount your suggestion at this point because I don't know enough about the victim. What other motive is there?" Kayli asked.

She saw her partner shrug out the corner of her eye. "No idea. Who knows why family members kill their kin sometimes? Could be all manner of reasons."

"Money?"

"It's possible. We don't know what state Paul's finances were in. Something we should look into when we get back to the station, perhaps?"

"Worth a shot. We looked into the backgrounds of each of the family members on our radar, and nothing showed up that should raise our suspicions with the kids as far as I can recall."

"I was thinking that. It's all a damn mystery. Let's hope Anita can start filling in some blanks for us when she wakes up, because at the moment, we're treading water and not getting very far."

Dave rang Donna. She told him that Dylan's vehicle was a Suzuki Jimny and supplied the registration number. They were ten minutes away from the siblings' house when Kayli's mobile rang. Using the Bluetooth connection, she answered the phone. "DI Bright speaking."

"Hello there, Inspector. This is Sylvia Addison, the manager from the Nightingale Care Home."

"Hello again, Mrs. Addison. What can I do for you?"

"When you left, I ran through what happened and realised I should have informed you about several strange things that have occurred around here lately."

"Strange? In what way?"

"We've had a few instances noted down regarding some of the residents complaining that money has gone missing—only a couple of people. We've also had a few incidents where patients have had valuables taken, such as jewellery and even cases where more medication has gone missing."

"Were these incidents investigated internally, or did you call the police in?"

"Unfortunately, as the incidents took place over the course of a year, we didn't really think anything of it. We investigated each case on its own merit and came to the conclusion that possibly the patients had either mislaid the items or given them to a family member to look after and forgotten doing that. A lot of our patients suffer from dementia, you see, Inspector."

"Or maybe someone used that fact to benefit from your patients. Did you question all the staff?"

"We did, and at the time, nothing untoward was highlighted. As I say, it's only since your visit earlier that my mind has revisited the incidents."

"Did you spot any links?"

"As it happens, yes. All the incidents took place when Sharon Potts was caring for those patients. I never made the connection at the time. Silly of me, I know. I suppose I'm just a trusting person by nature."

"Not everyone has a suspicious mind like me, Sylvia. Please don't be hard on yourself. Would you like to make a formal complaint now? It's not too late."

"That's why I was ringing up, to see if that would be acceptable or if there was a time limit on these things."

"I'll send a couple of constables over to take down a statement from you, if that's all right with you?"

"That would be fine. Shall I highlight the latest incident?"

"It makes sense to me. Thank you for getting in touch. The more we have on Sharon, the more likely we are to gain a conviction."

"It's a pleasure to help. I hope you catch up with her soon."

"So do I, Sylvia. At the moment, it looks like she's still running. Innocent people don't run. I'll get on to the station now for you." Kayli pushed the button on the dashboard to end the call.

"From that information, are we to surmise that Sharon is a greedy shit? And that she possibly killed her stepfather because of the money?" Dave asked.

Kayli drummed her fingers on the steering wheel. "I'm thinking we need to delve into the will side of things. Not only Paul's will, but also what was written in his wife's and how her estate was distributed. Maybe that's the trigger here."

Dave blew out a long breath. "If that turns out to be the case, they're nothing but a couple of twisted fuckers!"

"I'd add cunning to that accolade."

"You're right. The list is endless—conniving, manipulative, just plain evil."

"Yep, all of the above and so much more. Poor Anita. I wonder if she knew what her siblings were capable of."

"I doubt it. They're probably two-faced, as well, showing one side of their personas to Anita and another when they're in each other's company. Sick shits."

They drove the rest of the way each deep in thought.

"Okay, this is their road. I'll drive past at a normal speed to avoid raising any suspicions if they're at the property, on the lookout for us. Keep an eye out for the vehicles, both of them."

"What then? We call for backup and go in there?"

"That's the plan, partner. The last thing I want is the two of them escaping. We've had enough running around after Nuttall the last few days to last me a lifetime."

"True enough. I can't see anything yet. Hey, maybe there's a garage at the rear of the property. One of us should check that out before we leave."

"'One of us' meaning me, I take it?" she said, shaking her head.

"Well, I can hardly do it, can I?"

"Granted. I'm going to pull up at the end of the road and see if there's an alley that leads around the back."

Kayli parked in a large space and sprinted from the vehicle. She spotted a small pathway that led up the side of the row of terraced houses and took it. Her mouth was dry, and she swallowed nervously as she got to the end of the path. As far as she could make out, there were no garages to the properties. She ran back to the car. "Nothing. Okay, let's get back to the station and see if Graeme can pick up anything on the CCTV cameras in the vicinity of the pub."

~ ~ ~

They arrived at the station a short while after. Donna and Graeme were both hard at work when Kayli and Dave entered the incident room.

"Donna, can you get your hands on a copy of Maureen Potts's will for me?"

"I can try, boss. I might need to ring Samuel to get the name of the family solicitor who dealt with the will. Do you think he'll mind me disturbing him?"

"I'm sure he won't. Tell him you're ringing on my behalf."

Donna immediately picked up the phone.

Kayli stopped by Graeme's desk. "Anything?"

"I've got the Fiat following Potts's car going into Wales. I'm just trying to locate the car coming back across the border. Nothing as yet."

"Maybe they took the scenic route home after the deed was completed," Dave called out.

"He might have a point, Graeme. Sorry to put all this on you. It's a massive task. Can you do me a favour before getting back to that? Will you pull up the CCTV footage around the pub where Dylan works on Dave's screen? He can be trawling through that to save some time."

"I'll get on it now."

Kayli looked at the clock on the wall and expelled an exasperated breath. It was already four o'clock, and neither she nor Dave had stopped for lunch. She wasn't really hungry, but she was in dire need of a caffeine fix. She bought four cups of coffee and distributed them to her grateful team. Perching on the edge of a desk near the white-board, she looked at her team, proud of the effort they had poured into the investigation so far. She placed her half-drunk cup of coffee on the desk beside her and picked up the marker pen. She wrote down the significant clues they'd uncovered and stood back to think about what direction the case was likely to take next.

Suddenly, an idea entered her head. "Their phones…"

"What about them?" Dave responded.

"We can track their route via their phone data," Graeme was quick to fill in.

Kayli snapped her fingers and nodded. "That's right. Let me make a call to one of our tech guys and get the ball rolling on that." She ran into her office and placed the call. She managed to persuade the head of department to look into the case himself and get back to her right away. She emerged from the office and almost bumped into Graeme heading her way.

"What have you found?" she asked him.

"I've managed to identify both cars on the M5, heading south."

Excitement pumped through her veins. "Are they together?"

"No. They're only fifteen minutes apart, though."

"Good work. I wonder where they're heading."

"My guess is probably either Devon or Cornwall," Graeme said.

"Hmm… notorious holiday destinations. Maybe a possible family cottage?"

Graeme nodded. "Want me to ask Donna to do a search for that?"

"No. I think that will only waste time. I'll ring Samuel. He's bound to know." She returned to the office and sat on the edge of her desk while she rang. "Hello, Samuel. It's DI Bright. How's Anita? Has she come around yet?"

"Not yet, Inspector. I'm still very concerned. There's no colour in her usually rosy cheeks. I'm at a loss what to do."

"You're doing everything you can right now by being there to support her. Have you tried talking to her? It's often meant to aid the patient's recovery when they subconsciously hear a family member's voice."

"The nurse said something similar. I tried it for a little while, but I must admit I felt a little foolish."

"That's understandable. Can I ask you a question? It's to do with the case."

"Of course. Anything I can do to help. You only have to ask—you know that."

"Thanks. Can you tell me if the family has a holiday home in either Devon or Cornwall? Somewhere Paul and Maureen used to take the kids when they were growing up?"

"Yes, they do."

Kayli hopped off the desk and grasped a sheet of paper and a pen to jot down the information. "It's a long shot, I know, but I don't suppose you know the address?"

"Not off the top of my head. It's in Mevagissey, Cornwall. Can't remember the name of the road. The cottage is called Ivy Cottage, and it's a stone's throw from the town, if that helps. May I ask why?"

Up until now, she hadn't told Samuel that she suspected that Sharon and Dylan had killed his brother and attempted to kill his niece. That type of news, she preferred to tell someone in person. She had to think quickly for a plausible reason for requiring the information. "Just something that occurred to me. Thanks for the information. I'll be in touch soon. Don't forget to keep talking to Anita. I'll drop by and visit when I get a free moment."

"I will do, Inspector. Thank you."

Kayli ended the call and immediately called the operator to get the number for the local police station in the Mevagissey area. "Hi, sorry to trouble you. I'm DI Bright of the Avon and Somerset Constabulary. Would it be possible to speak to the person in charge, please?"

"I'm the duty officer, ma'am. Sergeant Brent at your service. This is a small community. Not much call for more than a few of us to be on duty at once," he informed her in a strong Cornish accent.

"I see. Thank you, Sergeant. It's good to speak to you. How well do you know the inhabitants of your community?"

"It's a small fishing village. We have a population of just over four thousand, so I suppose pretty well. Why do you ask?"

Kayli envisaged the man sitting up erect at his desk in his neatly pressed uniform, his buttons shining after being polished at the end of each shift. "Does that go for people who own holiday cottages in the area too?"

"Of course. Most of them have been coming here for years. When they're away, they let us know, and we keep a regular eye on their properties for them. If anything happens, like a suspected break-in, we give them a courtesy call immediately. Can't remember the last time I had to do that, however. Not much crime in this area as such."

"Maybe you know the residents who own Ivy Cottage. Apparently, it's close to the town centre."

"No maybe about it. That's Paul and Maureen's place, the Pottses. Why do you ask?"

"That's right. I need the address of the property, Sergeant."

"May I ask why?"

Kayli debated whether to tell the man as a gem of an idea festered in her mind. "I believe two members of the family are on their way to the cottage, and I need to get hold of them in connection to a case I'm working on at present. Is there a landline at the house? Do you know?"

"I don't think so. Let me take a look in the book we note all the holiday residents down in. Just a tick."

Kayli chewed her lip as the plan grew clearer in her mind.

Finally, the sergeant came back on the line. "Ah, here we are. No, the family said they all had mobile phones and refused to pay BT for a landline for twelve months of the year when they only use the cottage now and again. Do you have the family's mobile numbers? You could call them direct."

Kayli sighed. "You've caught me out. Sorry, I know the numbers, but it's a delicate situation, Sergeant."

"I'm listening. I'm sensing that you're unsure whether to trust me or not, Inspector. Can I just say that I've been serving in the local police force for nigh on twenty-five years with an unblemished record? I always put members of my community first and have achieved several awards for going above and beyond my duty. I've won two awards for saving the lives of a couple of members too, I might add."

Kayli swallowed, feeling like a scolded teenager after being caught scrumping apples. "I'm sorry. I didn't mean to cause any offence. Look, I'm just going to set off now. I'd much rather go over the details in person, if that's okay with you? How long will you be on duty?"

"I'll be here until five in the morning. I drew the short straw of overseeing the night shift today. It must be urgent if you're coming all the way down here."

"It is. I'm not sure how long it will take me. I'll see you in a couple of hours. One last thing. Can you give me the postcode of the station? It'll be easier for me to find."

He reeled off the postcode and said farewell. Kayli walked back into the incident room after pulling on her coat.

"Going somewhere?" Dave asked, leaning on his crutch to stand up.

"I am, but you're not. You stay here. I'm going down to Cornwall."

"What? At this hour of the day? Are you insane? You are aware it's going to take you about three and a half hours to get there, right?"

Kayli winced. She had predicted the journey would take her around two hours maximum. She almost changed her mind, but the thought of arresting Sharon and Dylan as soon as possible promptly shoved that idea aside. "I'm going, Dave, and there's no point you trying to talk me out of it. I want these bastards caught ASAP."

"I can understand that. Why don't we set off first thing in the morning?"

"Because I want to go now. I'm not asking you to come with me. I've been in touch with the local police sergeant, and he's aware that I'm going down there to meet him. He'll be the backup I need when I approach the cottage. There's no need for you to be worried about me. If the Taliban couldn't bring me down, then neither will Sharon and Dylan Potts."

"Really? You're going to sling that shit at us every time you put your life at risk? I thought better of you than that, boss."

Kayli's eyes widened. Dave was obviously livid, but she was shocked to hear him speak to her like that. "Don't hold back, Dave. Let me know what you really think of my idea."

Dave's head dropped onto his chest, and he slammed the pen he was holding onto the desk. "Pardon me for caring about what happens to you. I'm sure we're all thinking the same."

"Are you?" Kayli challenged Donna and Graeme.

"We trust your intuition, boss," Donna said. "However, I have to partially agree with Dave. I don't think you should go alone. Take one of us with you, if only to share the driving. You've had a pretty hectic day, and driving on the motorway all that way can have a devastating effect on your concentration levels."

Kayli smiled. "Guys, I know you mean well. I'm fine. The adrenaline has kicked in, and all I want to do now is bring these shits down before they either kill someone or put another person in hospital. I'm not arguing about this. I'm wasting valuable time. I'll keep in touch. I promise."

With that, Kayli marched out of the incident room.

CHAPTER THIRTEEN

After filling the car with petrol, Kayli headed down the M5 towards the West Country. Ten minutes into her journey, she plucked up the courage to ring Mark. After the way her team had reacted to the news of her imminent departure, she had a feeling that Mark was going to be equally livid about her decision. She braced herself before she dialled his mobile.

"Hello, love. It's only me."

"Hi. Is something wrong?" he asked immediately.

"Not really. I'm ringing up to say I probably won't be home tonight."

"What? Why? Do you have a night on the town with the girls planned?"

"Hardly. I haven't done that in ages. I'm on the case, love. If you must know, I'm on my way down to Cornwall."

"What? I take it Dave is with you."

Kayli sighed heavily. "No, he's not. I felt with his bum leg, he'd be more of a hindrance than a help. I'm alone. I'm not in any danger, so don't worry about me."

"Don't worry about you? You're crazy if you think that, love. Why are you going to Cornwall? Tell me the truth, Kayli."

"I'm following the two suspects down there. Please, don't start getting heavy-handed with me. I know what I'm doing. The local police are aware of the situation and are going to assist me."

Mark let out an agonised groan. "Christ, you can be such a pain in the arse. Let me come with you."

"No. You have your own job to attend tonight. I'm fine. Trust me. If I thought I was in any danger, I wouldn't be going. You have my word on that, love."

"You're insufferable at times. Stubborn beyond words. Okay, keep me informed when you can. I'll be thinking about you. Stay safe."

Her shoulders slumped in relief. The last thing she wanted was to fall out with him over what essentially was only her carrying out her job. "Thanks, love. You know I'll be careful. Have a good evening at work. I'll ring you when time permits."

"Make sure you do, and for goodness' sake, be careful."

"I will. I love you."

"Ditto. You know that."

Tears misted her eyes when she heard Mark hang up. She could tell he was angry about the choice she had made.

Kayli put an upbeat CD in the player, more to keep her concentration from wandering during the journey than anything else. The journey was longer than she had anticipated, and she experienced eye strain due to the amount of traffic driving with headlights on full beam in the opposite lane.

She entered the Mevagissey police station car park at eight forty-five, and Sergeant Brent was everything she'd expected him to be. He welcomed her with a friendly smile and poured her a cup of coffee in his office before she even had the chance to formally introduce herself. "I really appreciate this, Sergeant."

"Would it be too much trouble to fill me in on the details now, Inspector? Or would you rather leave it until the morning and get your head down at a local hotel for the night?"

"No, I'm fine. I'm buzzing, if the truth be told. Where do I begin? First of all, can I ask how long you have known the Potts family?"

"That's a very good question. I suppose the answer would be around fifteen to twenty years. They used to visit a couple of times every year when the kiddies were younger. Not so much now that they've all grown up and flown the nest. Even the grandparents used to come down a few times a year to stay at the cottage. It was so sad when they passed away in that accident. Then Paul told me that his wife had passed last year. Well, it floored me, if I'm honest. Lovely family, they were. Never any trouble. The kids were all well behaved, not like some of the brats that come down here from the larger cities."

Kayli ran a hand over her face, hesitating for a moment before she broke the news about Paul. "I'm sorry, but I have some dreadful news to share with you."

"Oh, what's that?" He sat forward in his chair.

"Paul Potts was found murdered a few days ago."

"What? Oh my, I can't believe anyone would do such a thing. He was such a kind man. How do you know it was murder, Inspector? Or was that a dumb question?"

"Not at all. His brother contacted me on Monday this week to report Paul missing. My team and I have been trying to solve the puzzle of his disappearance all week. Then his car was discovered in South Wales in a ravine, and his body was found in the boot of the car. Though Paul was likely unconscious when he was placed in the boot, he drowned in the fast-flowing river at the bottom of the ravine."

"Oh my, what an evil act. Do you have any clues as to who the murderer might be?"

Kayli took a sip of her coffee and nodded. "We have a fair idea."

"Aren't you going to share that information with me, Inspector?"

"If you insist. Prepare yourself for yet another shock. We believe two of his children are the culprits."

"That's ludicrous. Why would you say such a thing?"

Kayli sighed. "Their sister is at this moment lying in a hospital bed."

"Which one? Which sister?"

"Anita. At first, she was being treated as an attempted suicide patient, after she was found with a pot of pills lying beside her."

"Lordy, and you don't believe that's what truly happened to her? She was extremely close to her father, you know. Hang on a second... two children, you said? Are you insinuating that Sharon and Dylan killed their father?"

"Their stepfather, yes."

"I'm confused. What has led you to believe such a thing, Inspector?"

Kayli ran through the investigation with the sergeant. He shook his head in disbelief several times.

"It seems incredible that they would go to such lengths. Do you know why?"

"No. I've yet to establish that fact, although I have an inkling it's probably to do with money. My team are still looking at that aspect of the case. The thing is, if they're innocent, why would both of them flee? Neither of them had booked time off from work. They simply took off—Sharon while I was at the care home, waiting to speak to her. Suspicious, right?"

"I should say so. And you've followed them down here. Do you know they're coming here for definite?"

"No. It's a guess. A member of my team spotted both their vehicles heading this way on the motorway, and Paul's brother said the family had a holiday cottage in the area."

"You're a good detective, Inspector. Do you want to head out to the cottage now?"

Kayli nodded. "If only to check their vehicles are there."

"Then what?"

She tutted. "I'd like to arrest the pair of them. The trouble is that will be difficult if it's just the two of us, although I have brought along my trusty Taser, just in case."

"I can arrange for a couple of colleagues to join us. That wouldn't be a problem. I have a truncheon that comes in handy now and again." The sergeant chuckled.

"Excellent. I'll nip to the loo while you place the calls."

"First door on the left. Let's get this show on the road."

Within ten minutes, three of Sergeant Brent's colleagues had arrived. Each of them eyed Kayli warily until Brent painted the picture of what was going on for them.

Eager to get to the house, Kayli asked, "Is the property very far from here?"

"Not really. We'll go in two cars. All right, lads?"

The five of them left the station and hopped into two vehicles: one a police squad car and the other a Vauxhall Astra belonging to one of the officers. Kayli was alone with Sergeant Brent in his vehicle.

"I hope they don't offer any kind of resistance," she said, the palms of her hands becoming increasingly slippery the closer they got to the cottage.

"If they do, Inspector, you take a step back and leave them to us."

There's no fear of that happening, Sergeant! "We'll see. Hopefully, the element of surprise will mean they're unarmed."

"I know what you told me, but there is still an element of doubt about this whole scenario. No disrespect, ma'am."

"None taken. If, as you say, you've had nothing but positive interactions with the family in the past, then I can understand your reluctance to believe me even after all the evidence I've shared to the contrary. If this is all about the money, greed can be a powerful motivator in instances such as this. I've dealt with a few similar cases over the years, and they never end well for the person who committed the crimes."

"Glad to hear it. If these types of cases are prevalent, it makes you wonder how many of the bastards get away with it."

"In my experience, people have a tendency to slip up when it's least expected and often get found out in the end. That's what I prefer to believe, as it would be far too depressing to think otherwise."

"It's just around the corner here."

Kayli inhaled and exhaled a few times as the cottage they were after came into view. It was detached, with neighbours on either side. The houses were far enough apart to give each of the properties plenty of privacy without them feeling too remote. There were four lights on in the property. Kayli let out a sigh of relief. "They're here. Thank God I haven't had a wasted trip."

"Seems that way."

The pair of them left the vehicle and joined the other officers at the wooden gate leading to the property.

"Do you want to take the lead, Inspector?" Sergeant Brent asked. "Or would you rather I did?"

"I'm happy to go along with anything you suggest, Sergeant. I think the second the siblings lay eyes on me, they'll realise what's going on."

"I'll take the lead, then. Do you want to hang around at the back of the pack, so to speak?"

"Makes sense to me."

"Then onwards, men and lady. We have a couple of nasty villains to apprehend."

The five of them marched towards the house and up the narrow concrete path, an outdoor light close to the front door highlighting their surroundings. The pretty garden was well tended, and a lot of the rose bushes on either side of the path were still in full bloom. Kayli detected their scent as she walked. She hid herself behind two of the thickset officers as the sergeant rang the bell.

"Hello, Sergeant. What are you doing here?" Dylan asked in a confused tone.

"Hello, Dylan. Nice to see you again. Do you mind if we step inside for a moment?"

"Do I have any option? Actually, I do. Bugger off." Dylan tried to slam the door in their faces, but the officers surged forward.

The door slammed against the hall wall. Dylan tottered a little and ran the length of the hall and into a room at the end.

Kayli struggled to see what was going on and decided to leave the men in the house and try to find her way around to the back of the property. It was dark at the side of the house, and she caught her face on several overhanging bushes before she emerged into the back garden to find a bewildered Sharon looking at the house. "Hello, Sharon. There's no point running. It's over now. We know what you've done."

Dylan flew out of the back door and stood next to his sister. Holding a large kitchen knife in his hand, he glared at Kayli.

Kayli held out a hand. "It's pointless running. Why don't you put the knife down, and we'll talk about this, Dylan?"

"Some hope of me doing that, bitch." He glanced over his shoulder as the back door opened and the officers ran towards him.

"No! Stop!" Kayli ordered.

The men piled into each other as the front two stopped about four feet from Dylan. He reached for his sister's hand. Her gaze was shifting between the officers, her brother and Kayli. As Dylan looked at his sister and reassured her everything was going to be all right, Kayli removed her Taser from the back of her trousers and pointed it at him.

"Drop the knife, Dylan."

"Or what? You'll shoot me?" He laughed, an evil, ridiculing laugh that infuriated Kayli.

She had no hesitation in pulling the trigger. Dylan dropped to the ground as fifty thousand volts surged through his body. Sharon screamed and dropped to her knees beside her brother, unsure whether to touch him or not. She looked up at Kayli, her eyes narrowed as her lips thinned into a straight line in anger.

"You bitch. You've killed him."

"Hardly, Sharon. Cuff her, lads."

Kayli waited until both suspects were cuffed before she retrieved the Taser darts. She had released her hold on the trigger as soon as Dylan dropped to the ground, ensuring that the stun used was of minimum force. Pleased with her actions, she left the suspects and walked over to the sergeant. She held out her hand for him to shake.

"Looks like you didn't really need our help after all, Inspector." He smiled and winked at her.

"Nonsense. I couldn't have done it without your backup. Thank you to you and your colleagues. I need to get these two banged up in a cell overnight. Do you have the facilities to do that at the station?"

"No, I'm afraid not. Nearest large station is Saint Austell. I can escort the suspects there for you or get my colleagues to."

"That would be wonderful. I'll contact my station and arrange for them to be picked up first thing in the morning."

"What will you do now?"

"Find a cheap hotel for the evening and head back at dawn."

"I'll say this, Inspector. I've never had the honour of working alongside such a ballsy female officer as yourself. Do you have any fear?"

Kayli cringed. "Not sure whether to take that as a compliment or not." She leaned in close and whispered, "I recently whipped the Taliban's arse over in Afghanistan, so bringing these two down was a piece of cake."

His mouth dropped open. Kayli laughed and stepped away from the crowd to place the call to the station.

CHAPTER FOURTEEN

After ringing the station and arranging for a police van to pick up Sharon and Dylan Potts in the morning, Kayli found a small motel to rest her weary head for the night. She ate a swift meal of a chicken burger and chips in the restaurant then retired to her room. She had a quick shower, dried her hair then slipped into bed. Before her eyes began to droop, she sent a text message to Mark, telling him that the arrest had been made and that she was safely tucked up in a motel room. No sooner had she sent the message than her phone rang.

"You didn't have to ring me. I understand that you're busy, love."

"Nonsense. I cleared it with the boss beforehand. Glad you're safe. How did the arrest go?"

"It was eventful. Nothing too taxing compared to what we've recently had to endure. I'm going to get some sleep now. I want to be on the road at six. I'll drop by the house and get changed before I go into work."

Mark tutted. "You're a bloody workaholic. You should take the day off, the amount of hours you've put in today."

"You worry too much. I'll see you in the morning."

"I know when to stop nagging you." He sniggered. "Goodnight. Sleep well."

"I have a feeling I will. Love you." She hung up. But before she switched off the light, Kayli rang Dave. "Hi, it's me. A quick update for you."

"Are you all right? Where are you? Still in Cornwall?"

"Yes. The arrest has been made, and both suspects are sitting in a police cell in Saint Austell. I've rung our station, and they're sending a van to pick them up. I want to be on the road by six in the morning. Just wanted to let you know I might be a bit late into work. Pass that on to the DCI if she comes to hunt me down."

"Excellent news on the arrest. I can understand you wanting to be here tomorrow instead of taking the day off."

"Yep, I want to interview these two as soon as possible. Any news on the phones?"

"Before we left the office, the tech guy rang and said he could place both phones at the ravine where Potts's body was discovered. Bloody idiots—their intentions might have seemed clever to begin with, disposing of the body where it wasn't likely to be found for a while, but they didn't think to cover their tracks in other aspects."

"People look for the perfect murder, but very few ever think their plans through thoroughly enough to successfully achieve their aim. Or maybe it's a case of the A-Team being shit-hot again, Dave."

He laughed. "I'm willing to go along with you on the last part of your statement."

Kayli chuckled. "Okay, I'm hitting the sack now. Goodnight and see you in the morning."

"Gotcha. Well done, Kayli."

She ended the call, set the alarm for five thirty, plugged her phone to charge and snuggled down underneath the quilt.

~ ~ ~

The alarm going off made her pull her pillow over her head. "God, is it that time already?"

She groaned, switched the alarm off and shot out of bed and into the bathroom. With no toothbrush or toothpaste with her, she felt unclean as she hit the road. She took the packet of two complimentary biscuits with her to eat in case hunger struck on the long journey ahead.

At around nine thirty, she parked outside her home and entered the house quietly so as not to wake Mark. She needn't have bothered, because he was sitting up in bed, reading a car magazine when she popped her head into the room.

She blew him a kiss from the doorway. "I need to clean my teeth before I kiss you. You should be asleep anyway."

"I've only been awake for half an hour. I'll go back to sleep once you leave for work. It's good to see you in one piece."

"It's good to be home. Let me visit the bathroom, and we'll have a quick chat before I go."

"I'll nip and make us both a coffee."

She smiled at his thoughtfulness. When she came out of the bathroom a few minutes later, her mouth minty fresh, Mark was still pottering around downstairs. She went down to find him. "What are you doing? I don't have time for this."

Mark was standing at the stove, frying eggs and bacon in a pan.

"Nonsense. It'll take ten minutes for you to scoff this. Now sit!"

Kayli collapsed into the chair while he dished up the breakfast. "Are you not joining me? I feel really bad now."

"Nope. It's still the middle of the night for me. Don't feel bad. Just enjoy it."

Kayli was hungrier than she realised and wolfed down the breakfast in a matter of minutes, much to Mark's amusement. "That was delicious. You're definitely a better cook than me."

"Nonsense. It was bacon and eggs, for goodness' sake. So now that you've caught the suspects, will you be interviewing them today?"

"Yep. I'm hoping they'll be at the station by mid-morning. That gives me enough time to piece everything together and to hit them with the facts, although not all of them. I prefer to keep certain things concealed until the court case."

"I'll never understand how you manage to wrap a case up so quickly."

"It amazes me at times. I'm surrounded by the best team, and I suppose we're in tune with each other."

"You mean you rely on your team and treat them as equals, unlike other DIs."

She smiled and nodded. "It's definitely a team effort. Just like our marriage. Your support means everything to me, and I also appreciate that you're a dab hand in the kitchen too."

"Flattery will get you everywhere, Mrs. Wren." He leaned over to kiss her. Their lips met for a few fleeting moments before Kayli pulled away.

"I better get on the road. If I stay around here much longer... well, we both know what will happen."

She stood and tucked the chair under the table. "Leave the dishes in the sink. I'll do them when I get home later."

"Nope. I'll do them before I take to my bed. Have a good day and give the suspects hell from me."

She pecked him on the cheek and sprinted out the door. Kayli arrived at the station at five minutes to ten, much later than she had anticipated.

The team stood and applauded her the second she stepped into the incident room. "Hey, you lot can pat yourselves on the backs too. This case wouldn't have been solved so swiftly if you guys hadn't been on form."

"Thanks. We really appreciate that, boss," Donna called out, heading towards the vending machine. Then she deposited a cup of coffee on the desk next to Kayli.

"Thanks, Donna. Okay, any news on the suspects? The desk sergeant was on his break when I came through reception."

"I keep checking on their progress," Dave informed her. "They're about half an hour away."

"That's excellent news. Gives us time to pull the case together before the interviews begin."

"Who are you intending to start with?" her partner asked.

Kayli took a sip of coffee and thought over his question. "I thought I might give Dylan a shot first."

"You think he's going to be the tougher nut to crack?"

"Possibly. We'll soon see. Is the interview room ready, Dave?"

"All sorted. I made sure of that on the way in this morning to save my old legs a bit."

"Brilliant!"

They spent the next half an hour pulling together all the case notes and critical evidence. The desk sergeant rang her soon after they'd completed their task.

"I'm going to start the interviews right away, Sergeant. I'll see Dylan Potts first. Can you transfer him to the interview room? Dave and I will be down shortly."

"Yes, ma'am. The duty solicitor is waiting in reception too."

Kayli and Dave took their notebooks and Kayli's laptop downstairs, where they joined a male constable, Dylan Potts and the female duty solicitor in the interview room. Dylan's head remained bowed, his chin touching his chest, which was rising and falling rapidly, indicating that he was either nervous or full of rage.

Dave started the recording machine and said the usual, then Kayli took over. "Dylan, is there anything you want to say about the charges we have against you?"

"No comment."

Kayli rolled her eyes. "Is that how you're going to play this, Dylan?"

"No comment."

Every question or statement Kayli uttered after that was met with the same response. In the end, she gave up and instructed the constable to escort Dylan back to a cell and to bring Sharon back with him.

"I guess that was to be expected," the solicitor said.

Kayli nodded. "I suppose so. I'm warning you now that I won't let Sharon get away with doing the same."

The solicitor smiled. "I thought you might say something along those lines. Just don't overstep the mark, Inspector."

"I won't. Don't worry," Kayli replied.

The door opened, and a dishevelled Sharon walked into the room and slumped into the chair next to her solicitor. Again, Dave introduced everyone in the room and gave the date and time for the purpose of the recording machine before Kayli took up the reins and began the interview. Only this time, she opened up her laptop and pressed the Enter button. The footage Graeme had downloaded to her computer filled the screen. "Is that your car, Sharon?"

"It might be."

"What a coincidence! Isn't the jumper you're wearing driving the car the same that you have on today?"

"It might be," she repeated.

Kayli exhaled an impatient breath. "What about this?" She pointed to the screen at another car. "Perhaps you can tell me whose car that is, Sharon?"

"Nope, never seen it before!" she shouted before her head dropped onto her chest.

"Really? I would think very carefully before you start lying, Miss Potts. That car, as you well know, belongs to your stepfather, Paul Potts. Am I right?"

"You might be," Sharon said quietly.

"May I ask why you were following your stepfather's car that day?"

"Can't remember. Are you sure it's his car?" Raising her head, she looked Kayli in the eye and held her gaze defiantly.

"We're definite. Do you want to revisit your answer?"

"Not really."

"I put it to you that on Saturday, the twenty-fifth of November, you followed your stepfather's car over the border into South Wales. How am I doing so far?"

Sharon crossed her arms and shrugged. "Whatever."

"To a remote location where you and your brother, Dylan, jettisoned your stepfather's car over a ravine with your stepfather, who may have been unconscious, curled up in the boot of his vehicle."

Sharon's eyes narrowed. "Whatever. Prove it."

Kayli smiled. "We'll use your brother's statement, along with other critical evidence we have uncovered so far to do that in the courtroom itself. Do you want to revisit your answer, Sharon?" Kayli knew she was chancing her arm by bluffing about what Dylan had revealed, but past experience told her that sometimes the tactic worked when questioning more than one suspect, especially when there was a grave crime involved.

Her mouth dropped open for an instant then closed again. "He wouldn't!"

Kayli smiled and nodded. "He would, and he has." She avoided glancing in the solicitor's direction, though she saw the woman looking up from her notes in her peripheral vision.

"I don't believe you. Anyway, there's nothing to tell. Your assumption is wrong."

"Okay, let's leave that aspect of the case for a moment or two, shall we? Oh, before we do, did you get on well with your stepfather?"

"We tolerated each other," she snapped back quickly.

"Did you kill him because of the money?" Kayli pressed, deciding to stick with her line of enquiry after all.

The sudden rise and fall of Sharon's chest indicated her stress levels were on the increase. She made a guttural noise before she slammed her fists on the desk. Her face contorted with anger, and her cheeks went the shade of a ripe tomato. "He deserved it. They all did!"

"All? Meaning what? Are you referring to Anita, as well as someone else, in that sweeping statement?"

Sharon held her gaze once again before she tipped her head back and let out an evil laugh that chilled Kayli to the bone. "You're supposed to be the detective. Why don't you work it out for yourself?"

Kayli smiled, flicked through her notebook and sat back in her chair. "Okay, let's try this, for starters. Your grandparents, they died in a car accident, didn't they? I'm guessing that you and Dylan had something to do with that accident. You tampered with the car's brakes. How am I doing so far?"

Sharon shrugged.

Kayli pressed on. "Why? Because you expected some kind of inheritance bequeathed to you in their wills?"

Again, Sharon glared at her.

"Then there was your mother's tragic death due to cancer. I doubt you would have had anything to do with that, but I'm surmising that you were expecting her to treat you well in her will. Only she didn't. She left everything to Paul, didn't she? There's no point denying it. I've had access to the will and read it for myself."

Sharon sighed heavily and folded her arms tighter across her heaving chest but remained silent.

Kayli had the feeling Sharon was mulling over her options and decided to play her last card. "Then we move on to what went on with your stepsister, Anita, who, to my knowledge, is still unconscious in hospital after you tried to kill her."

Sharon shook her head, slowly at first, but the more Kayli stared at her, the more the shaking of her head increased. "I was helping her out. She wasn't sleeping."

"So you decided to steal a patient's tablets from the care home where you work and give them to Anita? Knowing the risks that action would carry? Is it advisable to give someone another person's medication without a doctor's authority? I don't think so. Why did you do it?"

Her look darkened in an instant, and her lip curled. "I was fed up with her crying over him. He was nothing. He promised us that we would have an equal share from Mum's estate, even though she left everything to him. The next week, he informed us that he'd bought that shitty house full of tenants who abused his trust."

"Do you know how ironic that last part of your sentence sounds? People who abused his trust! That's why you killed him and attempted to end Anita's life for her? So that you and Dylan could finally get what was owing to you in the form of inheritance?"

"Whatever. Read into it what you will. I'm not saying another word."

"You don't have to. The evidence is clear. You and Dylan hatched a plan that started with the deaths of your grandparents and ended with Anita almost losing her life."

She looked Kayli in the eye and sneered. "Shit happens."

Kayli shook her head when she witnessed the hatred deep within Sharon's eyes.

"I think we've heard enough. Constable, take Miss Potts back to her cell. You'll spend the next few hours here before you're transferred to a remand centre. I hope for your sake that Anita pulls through this, because at present, both you and Dylan are going down for three murders—Paul's and that of your grandparents. I'll also be adding an attempted murder charge to the list too."

Sharon's shoulders rose and almost covered her ears before they dropped again. "Whatever, like I'm bothered."

Kayli motioned for the constable to escort her from the room. After they left, Kayli let out a relieved sigh. "What a twisted bitch. Why the hell are some people so driven by money? If she and Dylan were that fond of it, why in God's name didn't they get out there and secure better jobs for themselves and start earning it like normal folks do? Bloody makes me so angry! It's as though there are some people walking the streets today who believe life owes them the world."

Dave nodded and tucked his notebook in his pocket. "They're a couple of nasty characters. That's for sure."

"It takes all sorts," the solicitor agreed.

EPILOGUE

Kayli received the call from Samuel at three o'clock that afternoon. She jumped in the car and headed to the hospital immediately. After flashing her ID at the uniformed officer guarding the private room, she barged in and smiled at Anita, who was sitting up in her bed, looking bewildered and confused.

"Hello, Inspector. It's good of you to come," Samuel said, appearing as if the weight of the world had lifted from his shoulders since she'd last seen him.

"Good to see you too, Samuel and Anita. How are you feeling?"

"My head doesn't feel like it belongs to me. Can you tell me what happened?"

Kayli sat in the chair close to Anita's bed and covered the young woman's cold hand with her own. "I was hoping you'd be able to fill us in."

"My head is filled with confusion. Did you come to tell me that Dad's body had been found?"

"I did. Can you remember anything else?"

"I remember Sharon showing up at the house. She was angry. I tried to calm her down when she…"

"When she what, Anita?"

The colour drained from her cheeks when she turned to face Kayli. "She said she had asked the doctor for some pills to help me sleep. I told her I wasn't keen on taking pills and refused to take them. Her anger scared me, but she produced a kitchen knife and ordered me to take a handful. When I refused a second time, she pounced on me, held the knife to my throat and forced me to take them." Anita began to sob.

"It's all right. You're safe now."

Anita's breathing came in short bursts. "She warned me that either I took the tablets, or she would slit my throat." Anita turned to

Samuel and reached for his hand. "Either way, she was going to kill me."

Kayli was still covering Anita's other hand, and she squeezed it reassuringly. "You're safe. We've arrested Dylan and Sharon. I'm sorry to have to tell you this, Anita, but they killed your father."

Anita turned to face her swiftly. "Why?"

"Because of the money. Greed on their part. We don't have the evidence yet, but I also believe that they killed your grandparents."

"But they died in a car crash."

"Accidents can be caused by a vehicle malfunctioning. I'll get the report looked over again to see what we can find. Anyway, Sharon virtually admitted it on tape during her interview this morning. I'm sorry you had to go through this trauma, Anita. I truly am."

"My family, all my family has disintegrated within a week."

Samuel cleared his throat. "Nonsense, love. You have me, and I'm not planning on going anywhere anytime soon. For a start, I want those two brought to justice first."

"Who knew? I know I didn't suspect anything. They've always been all right towards me. Although thinking back briefly, I can recall a couple of instances where I caught Sharon looking at me in an evil way." Anita shuddered.

"It's all over now. They can't hurt you again. I promise. I'll ensure they go away for a very long time indeed."

Anita and Samuel both smiled at Kayli and said *thank you* in unison. Kayli left the hospital and drove home. It was early to end her shift, but since she'd put in extra hours the day before, she felt entitled to go home and spend some time with her husband. She stopped off at the local butcher's to pick up a couple of fillet steaks for their dinner.

Mark was excited to see her home early, and they spent the next few hours together, preparing the meal and chatting about everything under the sun. When he left the house at eight o'clock, Kayli settled down on the couch and rang Giles. "Hi. How's everyone doing?"

"We're fine. I was going to ring you later."

"Oh, why?"

"To invite you and Mark round for Sunday lunch. Mum and Dad will be here."

"We'd love to come. What time?"

"Be here around one, or before, if you want to lend a hand in the kitchen."

Kayli laughed. "Gosh, you must be desperate if you want me to help out in the kitchen. Does this mean you'll be cooking?"

"Yep. I volunteered, and I'm kind of regretting that decision now. Do you have any idea of the amount of work involved in throwing together a roast dinner for seven people?"

"Idiot. Mark and I will be there around ten to assist you, oh hopeless one."

"You sound cheerful."

"Yes and no. We wrapped up the case I was working on, so I came home early to spend some time with Mark before he left for work."

"That's great news. Sorry you guys are working opposite shifts. Hope that works out better for you both soon. See you on Sunday then, bright and early."

"Well, ten o'clock as agreed," she corrected him before ending the call.

~ ~ ~

On Sunday morning, Kayli and Mark turned up at her brother's house, laden with bottles of wine. Although Giles had been his normal cheery self on the phone, she had no idea what kind of reception she was about to receive from Annabelle. Her concerns were unwarranted, however.

Annabelle hugged her tightly the minute she laid eyes on her and whispered in her ear, "I know what's going through your mind, and I want you to stop it right now. There is no way either of you are to blame for me losing the baby, so get that thought out of your head."

Kayli squeezed her tightly then released her. With tears misting her eyes, she touched Annabelle on the cheek. "You're such a caring person, love, always putting others' feelings before your own. Yes, you're right—I do feel guilty. But I want you to know that if you ever want to discuss the baby, it's all right with me. Please, whatever you do, don't ever feel the need to brush your feelings under the carpet."

"I won't. I promise."

"After all, we're a loving family who fight for each other. Through good times and bad, we stick with each other."

"That's pretty profound. Is everything all right, Kayli?" Annabelle asked with a concerned expression.

"I've just solved a pretty shitty case, and all it did, really, was highlight how much you guys and our family unit mean to me."

Annabelle hugged her again. "No one could ever doubt that after the great lengths you went to get Mark back."

"I know. It doesn't hurt to tell you guys now and again, though."

The day was filled with tender moments of love and laughter. It was the tonic they all needed to move on with their lives, knowing that their family bond was as solid as ever.

THE END

M A Comley

NOTE TO THE READER

Dear Reader,

What an exhaustive ride that was! I'm sure glad Kayli returned to save the day.

Kayli and the team will be back later in the year to solve more heinous crimes, I hope you'll join them.

For more fast-paced thrillers from my backlist why not try the intention series which begins with:

http://melcomley.blogspot.co.uk/p/sole-intention.html

Grab your copy today, it's available on all sites.

Thank you as always for reading my work, reviews are always welcome and a privilege to receive.

M A Comley

Made in the USA
San Bernardino, CA
19 June 2018